INTERNET DETECTIVES

ELECTRONIC MAIL

File   Edit   View   Options   Window   Utilities   Favelist   Help

From: Sent:
To: Subject:

michael coleman

CYBER FEUD

OPEN   SEND   FORWARD   REPLY   DELETE   SAVE   PRINT

Mail:

A WORKING PARTNERS BOOK

MACMILLAN CHILDREN'S BOOKS

First published 1996 by Macmillan Children's Books
a division of Macmillan Publishers Limited
25 Eccleston Place, London SW1W 9NF
and Basingstoke

Associated companies throughout the world

Created by Working Partners Limited
London W6 0HE

ISBN 0 330 34737 3

Copyright © Working Partners Limited 1996
Computer graphics by Jason Levy

9 8 7 6 5 4 3 2 1

A CIP catalogue record for this book is available from
the British Library.

Printed by Mackays of Chatham plc, Kent

CHAPTER 1

Abbey School, England.
Monday 1st April, 8.16 a.m.

With an easy movement, Josh slid the cursor up to the menu bar and clicked on 'Favelist'. Immediately, a drop-down menu of his favourite Internet destinations appeared. Josh clicked on 'Fun Fact', taking him to a site which offered a different snippet of trivia every day.

'April Fool's Day,' muttered Josh. 'It's April Fool's Day! How could I have forgotten that!'

He checked his watch. Yes, he just about had enough time …

8.29 a.m.
Tamsyn breezed in through the school gates and headed straight for the Technology Block.

Usually the double doors of the squat, red-brick building were visible. For the past two months, though, they'd been hidden beneath a makeshift porch of plywood and polythene, as the new Technology Block Extension took shape. And so it wasn't until she turned past a section of ground marked off with orange tape that the doors came into view – and she saw Josh.

He looked awful, as though he'd received a terrible shock.

'Tamsyn …' Josh shook his head in despair.

'What? What's wrong?'

'It's … it's gone!'

'Gone? What are you talking about, Josh? What's gone?'

Josh paused, running a hand through his spiky thatch of hair as if he was trying to think of the right words to use.

'The – the hard disk on the Computer Club's PC. Somebody must have got in over the weekend. The control unit's open and the disk has gone!'

He shook his head again. 'I was just on my way

to tell Mr Findlay. Your *Great Expectations* file. All your work ... all *our* work.'

Only as Josh mentioned the name of the famous book by Charles Dickens did the full impact of what had happened sink in. Charles Dickens was her favourite author, and she'd chosen his book *Great Expectations* to study for her English project.

She'd downloaded a copy of the book from the Internet and put it into a file on that disk. What's more, she'd spent hours and hours word-processing her own thoughts and comments into the middle of it.

And she hadn't taken a back-up copy. She'd meant to. Time and time again she'd told herself to bring a diskette and make a copy, but she'd always forgotten or run out of time or ...

'My file!' she wailed.

Josh gave her a glimmer of hope. 'I was on my way to tell Mr Findlay. He's got to know about the robbery. And I thought, maybe he's taken a back-up recently.'

'Mr Findlay!' It was a slim chance, but Tamsyn grabbed it eagerly. Mr Findlay was Abbey School's head of Design and Technology. The computers and their Internet link were his responsibility. Josh could be right. Maybe he'd have a back-up copy of the hard disk.

She thrust her shoulder bag into Josh's hands. 'You stay. I'll go find him!'

And before Josh could say a word she was off, her short dark hair flying as she ran.

She met Rob Zanelli on the way. Confined to a wheelchair after a car accident when he was eight years old, Rob was the third member of the group. Between them, they'd managed to crack a few mysteries over the Internet. And, as Tamsyn rushed towards him, it looked to Rob as though there might be another mystery looming.

'Tamsyn! What's up?'

'Computer Club PC,' cried Tamsyn without stopping. 'Hard disk stolen! All my Dickens work!'

Rob frowned. 'Are you sure?' he called after her.

'Ask Josh!' she yelled back. 'I'm going to get Mr Findlay!'

Tamsyn raced on, past a group of startled first-year kids and into the main building. Mr Findlay was just emerging from the Staff Room. Breathlessly, she told him what had happened.

'Are you sure?' he said.

The same daft question Rob had asked! 'Josh discovered it this morning,' she yelled. 'I've lost stacks of work!'

Mr Findlay's eyebrows arched. 'Sounds like I'd better see for myself,' he said solemnly. 'Hang on there for a minute.'

The teacher disappeared into the staff room, leaving Tamsyn waiting impatiently until he came out again a few seconds later with a buff folder under his arm.

'Right, Tamsyn. Lead on.'

Tamsyn hurried on ahead. Behind her, his keys

jangling musically from a clip on his belt, Mr Findlay followed – though not as quickly as she'd have liked. *Come on,* she thought as she stopped at the Technology Block doors to wait for him to catch up. *I know you're old, but you're not that old!*

When he finally arrived she just had to ask, 'Did you take a back-up of the disk, sir?'

Mr Findlay shook his head slowly. Tamsyn groaned. *All that work!* As they headed down to the end of the corridor, the thought of re-doing it all was making her feel ill.

As she raced ahead of Mr Findlay again, and elbowed her way through the door marked 'Computer Club', she failed to realize that Josh and Rob were both looking at her and grinning.

Only when they chimed together, 'April Fool!' did it fully sink in.

She closed her eyes. Feelings of relief mixed with feelings of stupidity. April the First! That's why Rob had asked if she was sure. That's why Mr Findlay had asked the same question.

'You toad!' she screeched at Josh. 'You weasel! You rat! You slimy—'

'Ah-ah,' said Mr Findlay, behind her. 'Tamsyn, I think you're going to have to accept it. You've been seriously fooled.'

Josh held up a diskette. 'Perhaps this will teach you to take back-up copies of your work, Miss Smith! Here you are. I've done one for you ...' His serious expression collapsed in a fit of the giggles. '... Be sure to write the date on it!'

'I'll write the date on *you*, Josh Allan – with the point of my compass!'

'If you don't mind leaving your acts of retribution until later, Tamsyn,' said Mr Findlay, edging into the computer room, 'I'd like a quick chat with the three of you.'

Tamsyn settled for giving Josh a jab in the ribs, then sat down next to him. Mr Findlay pulled a chair across from one of the desks and parked it beside Rob.

'How do you keep these two in order, Rob?' he said.

Rob grinned. 'It's not easy.'

'Well, if it's any consolation, they were a lot worse before you came. At least Tasmyn's a computer fan nowadays.'

They all knew what Mr Findlay was referring to. Rob had only joined Abbey School after an adventure in which Tamsyn and Josh had come to his rescue through Rob contacting them over the Net. In those days, Tamsyn hadn't liked computers at all.

Mr Findlay held up the buff folder he'd retrieved from the staff room. 'I assume you all remember this?'

Tamsyn was momentarily surprised to see her own neat handwriting on the front. And then she realized. 'Our Internet report,' she said.

When Abbey School first installed their Internet link, Tamsyn and Josh had been given the job of writing a report on its advantages and disadvantages. Rob had helped them finish it off when he'd started at the school.

'I was looking at it again over the weekend,' said Mr Findlay. He flipped over the pages. 'Especially this bit.' He read aloud the section he was referring to.

> *Being on the Internet means we can 'visit' lots of other computers and get information from them. But it also means that other people could 'visit' us, if we set up our own pages for them to read.*
>
> *This would be a good thing for Abbey School, because there are millions of people all over the world who are connected to the Internet, including lots of schools. They could all use our pages to find out about us and what we do here.*
>
> *We would be putting Abbey School into cyberspace. We could call it Cyber-Abbey!*

'I think that's a really good idea,' said Mr Findlay, closing the report. 'And now we've been on the Internet for a while, I think it's time we took up your suggestion.'

'For some Cyber-Abbey pages?' said Josh. 'Cool!'

'I hope you'll still think so when you hear my suggestion, Josh. I'd like you, Tamsyn and Rob to think about what sort of information we could include.'

'Right on,' said Rob at once.

'No problem!' said Tamsyn, just as enthusiastic as the two boys.

'Ideally, I'd like some thoughts by Friday the twelfth.'

'Why's that, Mr Findlay?' asked Rob innocently. 'Important day or something, is it?'

Mr Findlay raised the folder as if to clout Rob on the head. 'As you well know, Friday the twelfth is the day the Technology Block extension is being officially opened. There are going to be displays of all sorts, and I'd like to include one with your ideas.'

Rob, Tamsyn and Josh exchanged glances – and nods. 'Friday the twelfth it is,' said Tamsyn.

Abbey School. 12.40 p.m.

'So,' said Tamsyn, 'anybody had a bright idea?'

'I had one on the way to French,' said Rob, tucking into his lunchtime sandwich. 'I thought we could have a computerized plan of the school. When a user clicks on different spots, photos come up showing how it really looks.'

'Not bad. How about you, Techno-man?'

Josh grinned. 'Get this. The Abbey Cyber-Joke Centre. Visit our site for the best jokes in Cyberspace!'

'Very educational,' said Tamsyn. 'With me as the prize exhibit, I suppose?'

'Of course,' said Josh. 'What about you, then? Any brainwaves?'

'Nope,' said Tamsyn. 'But then I didn't try …' she added quickly as Josh put on his I-thought-not look, '… because my idea is to let the Net do the work.'

Rob looked at her. 'Check out some other

school sites, you mean? See if they've got anything we could copy? Good thinking.'

'So what are we waiting for?' said Josh, press-
ing the button on the front of the Computer
Club's PC. 'Let's go surfing!'

Within moments he was going through the
opening sequence which connected them to the
whole world-wide Internet network.

He sat up straight as, the initial flurry of activ-
ity over, the first menu screen flashed up. 'Aha!
Mail for me time!'

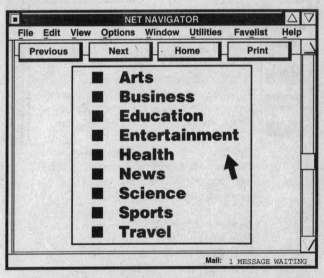

In the bottom right-hand corner of the screen,
on the status line, the words: MAIL: 1 MESSAGE
WAITING were flashing.

'I thought we were checking out school sites?'
said Rob.

'We are,' said Josh. 'Just as soon as I've read this.' He clicked on the OPEN button. Immediately the unread e-mail was displayed for him.

It was from Tom Peterson, their friend who lived in Perth, Australia. As usual, the note was copied to all three of them.

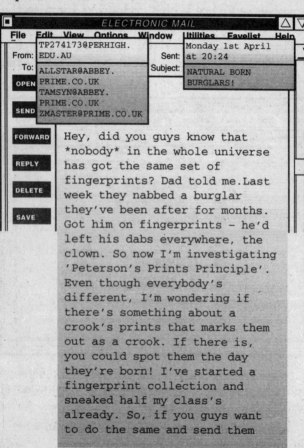

ELECTRONIC MAIL	△ ▽

File Edit View Options Window Utilities Favelist Help

From: TP274173@PERHIGH.EDU.AU Sent: Monday 1st April at 20:24

To: ALLSTAR@ABBEY.PRIME.CO.UK Subject: NATURAL BORN BURGLARS!
TAMSYN@ABBEY.PRIME.CO.UK
ZMASTER@PRIME.CO.UK

OPEN
SEND
FORWARD
REPLY
DELETE
SAVE

Hey, did you guys know that
nobody in the whole universe
has got the same set of
fingerprints? Dad told me.Last
week they nabbed a burglar
they've been after for months.
Got him on fingerprints - he'd
left his dabs everywhere, the
clown. So now I'm investigating
'Peterson's Prints Principle'.
Even though everybody's
different, I'm wondering if
there's something about a
crook's prints that marks them
out as a crook. If there is,
you could spot them the day
they're born! I've started a
fingerprint collection and
sneaked half my class's
already. So, if you guys want
to do the same and send them

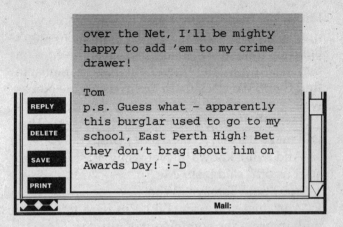

over the Net, I'll be mighty
happy to add 'em to my crime
drawer!

Tom
p.s. Guess what – apparently
this burglar used to go to my
school, East Perth High! Bet
they don't brag about him on
Awards Day! :-D

REPLY

DELETE

SAVE

PRINT

Mail:

Automatically, Josh clicked on the SAVE button to file the note away in his e-mail log in case he wanted to read it again.

'Hey, what about that?' said Rob, pointing at Tom's note.

Tamsyn laughed. 'That's what comes of having a detective for a dad.'

'No, for our Abbey Site project. We could build up a database on past pupils.'

'A crooks file, you mean? Ex-Abbeyites who've been banged up?' Tamsyn pulled a face. 'Mr Findlay will go a bundle on *that*!'

'Not crooks,' said Rob. 'Well, not *just* crooks. A file about *any* past pupil of the Abbey.'

Tamsyn sounded uncertain. 'Rob, that's a lot of people. This school has been open forty years! We'd have to get addresses, write letters and all sorts. It could take ages. We really need to have something we can do by

Friday the twelfth, don't we?'

'Use the Net!' cried Josh. 'It's perfect. We don't build up data on *all* past pupils – just the ones on the Net. And we don't send out snail-mail post to find them. We track them down using the Net as well.'

'Josh, that's a great idea,' said Tamsyn. 'That will make it a real Cyber-Abbey project!'

'And who knows a Net-using past pupil to start us off?' said Josh. 'Me.'

'You?' said Tamsyn. 'Who?'

'Aha! Just you wait. I'll be in here tomorrow with information coming out of my ears.'

Josh's House. Monday 1st April, 4.55 p.m.

The person Josh had been thinking of was Mrs Allan – his mum.

She worked part-time as a receptionist at a Health Centre, and they were about to go on-line ... which was close enough to being a Net user as far as Josh was concerned. Much more importantly, though, she used to *go* to Abbey School.

'Mum, when were you at Abbey?' he asked almost before he'd got in the door.

'Oh, Josh,' said Mrs Allan. 'I don't want to think about it. It must have been ... good heavens, nearly thirty years ago!'

'What was it like then?'

His mum shook her head. '*Very* different ...'

'What, black-and-white computer screens?'

'Computer screens? Josh, you're joking!

Nobody had computers in those days. Design and Technology meant art and woodwork, full stop. And the girls weren't allowed to do woodwork, either. We had cookery and that was that!'

Josh's nose caught the delicious smells wafting from the kitchen. *I'm not complaining,* he thought.

'Then, when we were in the fifth year – that's called year eleven, nowadays,' Mrs Allan continued, 'we all got to do a new-fangled subject called Electronics, where we messed about with wires and soldering irons and circuit boards. Great fun!'

Josh couldn't stop himself laughing. 'Electronics? A new subject?'

'Then it was. Mr Findlay introduced it. He'd only just started at the Abbey then. In fact, I think he's probably the only teacher who's left from my time.'

Mrs Allan opened the living room door. 'Hang on, I'll show you something ...'

As his mum went up the stairs to her bedroom, Josh did a bit of mental arithmetic. If she'd started at the Abbey thirty years ago, and Mr Findlay had joined when she was in the fifth form ...

'So old Findlay's been at the Abbey for twenty-five years?' he asked as his mum came back.

Mrs Allan was carrying an old square box, bulging at the seams. 'I suppose he has,' she said as she dropped it on to the kitchen table with a thump. 'Yes – this must be his anniversary year. Here you are, look.'

Josh's mum took the lid off the box and, from

the middle of a pile of clutter that made Josh wonder how come it was only *him* who was always being told how untidy he was, pulled out a short cardboard tube. From inside, Mrs Allan extracted a rolled-up photograph. Laying it on the dining table, she unwound it. The photograph was the best part of a metre in length.

'There he is,' said Mrs Allan.

Josh looked. The teachers were in the centre of the picture, seated on chairs.

'That's Mr Findlay?' Looking closer, he could see it was. His hair was much darker, but his unmistakable wry smile gave him away.

'So where are you?' asked Josh.

'Third row,' said Mrs Allan. 'Fourth from the left.'

Josh found her at once. 'Never! Much too pretty!'

'Cheek!' laughed his mum. She looked up at the sound of the front door opening.

Josh didn't hear it. Having found his mum, he was gazing at some of the other youthful faces in the picture. One in particular caught his eye. It couldn't be, surely? But it really looked like him …

'Hey, that's Dad, isn't it?'

Suddenly, Mrs Allan looked flustered. 'Er …'

Before she could answer, Josh's father breezed in. 'What're you two up to, then?'

Josh asked his question again. 'Mum was showing me her old school photo.' He pointed at the face in the picture. 'And isn't this you? I never knew you went to the Abbey.'

For the briefest moment, Josh's parents exchanged glances. Mr Allan's smile had faded as he came and stood at Josh's shoulder.

'I didn't,' he said.

Josh pointed. 'But, Dad, that has *got* to be you. Look at that hair!'

Mr Allan snorted. 'I know my own face, son,' he said. 'Anyway, how could it be me? I told you, I didn't go to Abbey School.'

It was his turn to ferret in the box. He pulled out a single sheet of school report. It had a crest emblazoned at the top. 'See. I went to Maylands.'

He then pulled another sheet from the box. 'There you are, that's the list of the Abbey School leavers that year. Am I on it?'

Josh shook his head. His mum's name was there, but not his dad's.

Josh wandered upstairs soon after. As he lay on his bed, idly looking at the class list, it didn't occur to him that he hadn't actually got round to asking his parents if they knew any ex-Abbeyites who were on the Net. All he could do was turn over and over in his mind what he'd just seen and heard.

And, try as he might, he couldn't get rid of the feeling that his parents hadn't been telling him the whole truth.

CHAPTER 2

Manor House, Portsmouth.
Tuesday 2nd April, 7.44 a.m.

Rob held a slice of toast in his right hand as he slid his computer's mouse with his left. A bite and a click later, the toast had gone and he'd opened the e-mail he'd just received.

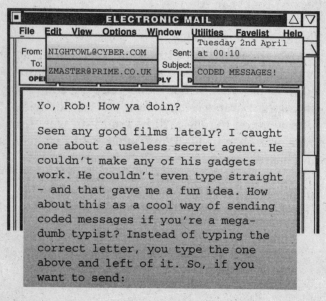

ELECTRONIC MAIL

File   Edit   View   Options   Window   Utilities   Favelist   Help

From: NIGHTOWL@CYBER.COM   Sent: Tuesday 2nd April
To: ZMASTER@PRIME.CO.UK   Subject: at 00:10
OPEN   PLY D   CODED MESSAGES!

Yo, Rob! How ya doin?

Seen any good films lately? I caught one about a useless secret agent. He couldn't make any of his gadgets work. He couldn't even type straight - and that gave me a fun idea. How about this as a cool way of sending coded messages if you're a mega-dumb typist? Instead of typing the correct letter, you type the one above and left of it. So, if you want to send:

```
TOP SECRET MESSAGE

What you actually type is:

590 W3D435 J3WWQT3

D'you reckon there are any crime-
busters out there who'd pay me a few
bucks for the idea?

Mitch

p.s. D9068HT 5Y8W 59 59J - Y3'OO
O9F3 85!
```

Mail:

Rob looked at the time the e-mail was sent. Ten
minutes past midnight. No wonder Mitch's Net
ID was NIGHTOWL!

Mitch lived in New York and worked part-time
in a café called Cyber-Snax, where customers
could Net-surf while they drank coffee. As Mitch
was allowed to log in when the place was shut,
his e-mails were usually sent at *very* odd times.

They also regularly contained all sorts of odd
ideas, such as this one. Grinning broadly, Rob
deciphered the line at the bottom. Reversing the
trick, and typing the characters on his keyboard
which were below and to the right of the one in
Mitch's line, he saw the result:

COPYING THIS TO TOM - HE'LL LOVE IT!

Rob laughed out loud. Mitch was right. Tom *would* love it!

Abbey School. 8.25 a.m.

Josh hit the power-on button on the front of the PC and settled down, waiting for it to finish its boot sequence. Then, as he got the Program Controller screen, he clicked on the globe-shaped Internet icon. He typed in his User ID and password, JOSHUA. After a short pause, he knew, the Internet start page would come up. Then he'd be on for some uninterrupted surfing before Tamsyn and Rob arrived.

But the Internet start page didn't come up. Instead, Josh was presented with a very different screen.

There'd been a system message about it recently. After a hacker had discovered a user's password and logged in under their name, a new security feature had been introduced. Now, users had to change their password regularly – and his had just reached its sell-by date!

Josh paused. *What should it be?* Something he could remember easily again, he decided.

He typed: JOSHING.

Immediately the system came back with the message:

Rats! thought Josh. He read the advice note. A mixture of letters and digits? If it got him over this irritating hurdle and onto the Net he'd try anything!

Quickly, and completely at random, he typed: X42ABN6.

Success! He tapped it in a second time and almost immediately got a simple message saying PASSWORD CHANGED. There was a short pause and then he was in and the Net start page was on the screen in front of him.

Josh was about to start surfing when he paused. The new password he'd just typed in – what had it been? X42ABN6, that was it. But would he remember it tomorrow? Mixtures of letters and digits might be unguessable, but they were also pretty unmemorable as well. JOSHUA had been no trouble – but X42ABN6?

Josh plucked a pen from his bag. Moments later, and looking like a clear blue tattoo, the legend X42ABN6 had been written on the back of his left hand. He would stare at it all day. Then, when he was sure he'd committed it to memory, he'd wash it off – or not wash for two months ...

8.36 a.m.

Tamsyn broke into a trot as she saw Mrs Zanelli swing her large estate car round in front of the school gates. By the time she reached it, Rob's wheelchair had been unloaded from the back and he'd slipped smoothly into it from the car's passenger seat.

'I got a nutty note from Mitch this morning,'

said Rob as they headed across towards the Technology Block. He told Tamsyn about Mitch's coded message idea.

'That sounds neat!' Tamsyn said.

Rob's wheelchair clonked against a large lump of brick, causing him to stop, reverse, and go round it. 'Which is more than can be said for this place!' he said.

The Technology Block Extension was virtually complete but the site still looked a mess. To their left, just beyond the fluttering orange tape, a large mound of rubble had been heaped up. Rust-coloured bits of stone and brick stood out against a brown background of earth. Tamsyn picked up the lump of brick and tossed it back onto the mound.

'Tidying up is the last thing they'll do, I reckon,' she said. 'Still, it'll have to be done soon. They won't want the Lord Mayor or whoever's opening the extension to fall flat on their face, will they?'

Heading on into the Technology Block, they reached Josh just as he'd finally managed to get onto the Net. He was in the middle of reading an e-mail he'd received from Lauren King. Lauren lived in Toronto, Canada, with her grandmother, Alice.

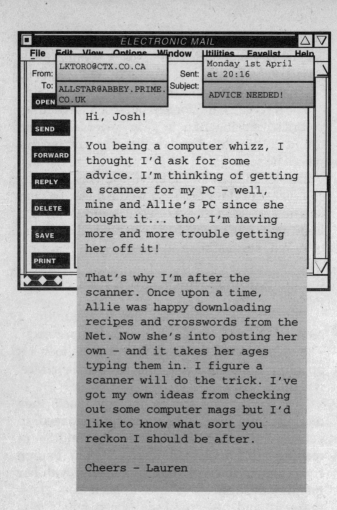

From: LKTORO@CTX.CO.CA

To: ALLSTAR@ABBEY.PRIME.CO.UK

Sent: Monday 1st April at 20:16

Subject: ADVICE NEEDED!

OPEN

SEND

FORWARD

REPLY

DELETE

SAVE

PRINT

Hi, Josh!

You being a computer whizz, I thought I'd ask for some advice. I'm thinking of getting a scanner for my PC — well, mine and Allie's PC since she bought it... tho' I'm having more and more trouble getting her off it!

That's why I'm after the scanner. Once upon a time, Allie was happy downloading recipes and crosswords from the Net. Now she's into posting her own — and it takes her ages typing them in. I figure a scanner will do the trick. I've got my own ideas from checking out some computer mags but I'd like to know what sort you reckon I should be after.

Cheers — Lauren

'A jet-propelled one by the sound of it,' laughed Rob, easing his wheelchair round to Josh's side.

Josh hit the REPLY button.

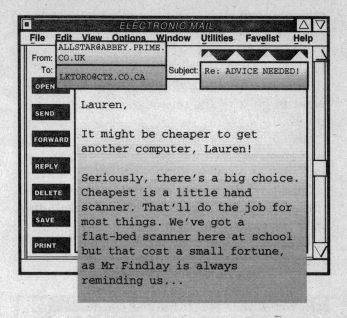

File Edit View Options Window Utilities Favelist Help

From: ALLSTAR@ABBEY.PRIME.CO.UK

To: LKTORO@CTX.CO.CA

Subject: Re: ADVICE NEEDED!

OPEN
SEND
FORWARD
REPLY
DELETE
SAVE
PRINT

Lauren,

It might be cheaper to get another computer, Lauren!

Seriously, there's a big choice. Cheapest is a little hand scanner. That'll do the job for most things. We've got a flat-bed scanner here at school but that cost a small fortune, as Mr Findlay is always reminding us...

'Talking of Mr Findlay,' said Rob as Josh hit SEND to launch his reply, 'where's that helpful info you promised?'

'It's to do with Findlay, actually,' said Josh. 'Did you know he's been here twenty-five years?'

'Only twenty-five?' said Tamsyn. 'Seems like two hundred!'

'So my mum was telling me, anyway.' The nagging thought that there'd been something that she, and his dad, *hadn't* been telling him crossed Josh's mind for a moment before he went on. 'Maybe we could use that.'

'What, put some stuff on about what life was like here twenty-five years ago?' said Tamsyn.

'That's not a bad idea. Not exactly high-tech, but not bad.'

'We could bring it all out at the Grand Opening,' said Josh. 'I'd love to see his face!'

'If we *can* find out anything,' said Rob. 'I still want to go with the idea about contacting past pupils.'

Josh opened his hands like a magician. 'Maybe we can do both. We can ask anybody we do contact what life was like at Abbey then.'

Tamsyn slid across to one of the other PCs and turned it on. 'Isn't there a better way of finding out?' she said.

Quickly, she went to the NET NAVIGATOR home page.

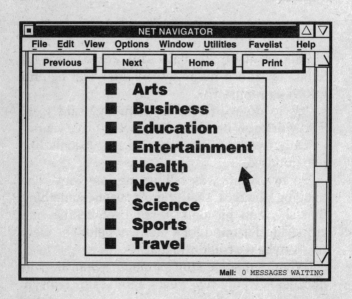

Clicking on the menu item NEWS produced another menu. This had FOREIGN, NATIONAL and LOCAL in it. Tamsyn highlighted LOCAL, then moved down to a panel at the bottom of the screen.

SEARCH FOR?

Tamsyn typed ABBEY SCHOOL, hit the RETURN key – and waited while the system searched all of the local news sources that were on the Internet for any reference to their school.

'Phew!' she said when she saw the outcome.

Search Results
Found 74 matches containing **ABBEY SCHOOL**.

The rest of the screen, and those that followed, listed every news reference to the school that had been found.

'Seventy-four of them!' said Josh. 'It'll take all the time we have to go through that lot!'

'Only if they're useful,' said Rob. He pointed at the first on the list. 'Hey, try the first one. It's got today's date on it.'

1. Tech. Block extension for **Abbey School**

Tamsyn clicked on it. After a short pause a small item from an on-line version of the local newspaper, the *Portsmouth Chronicle*, appeared on the screen.

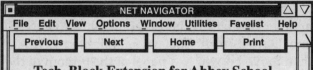
Tech. Block Extension for Abbey School
Paul Barrett to perform opening ceremony

Debbie Grant reports:
Abbey School's preparations for the 21st century will take a major step forward on 12th April with the opening of a large, purpose-built extension to their already impressive Technology Block.

The opening ceremony will be performed by local businessman and city councillor, Mr Paul Barrett.

'I am delighted and proud to have been asked,' Mr Barrett said from his offices in Northern Parade. 'As an ex-Abbey pupil myself I know what a tremendous school it is. It certainly gave me a great start in life twenty-five years ago.'

Modestly, Paul Barrett didn't mention his own superb achievement at that time in winning a prestigious scholarship with the electronics giant, Edison. Not only did he beat tough opposition from across the country, he scored 96% – still the highest mark ever obtained in the scholarship examination. The success guaranteed a job with Edison, and set him on the road to forming his own company twelve years ago.

And all this, I discovered, in spite of another difficulty. Paul Barrett had to take the examinations in the midst of chaos. Just a day before, a fire had broken out in a temporary classroom. But for prompt action by the emergency services the whole school could have burnt down – quite the opposite to the blaze of glory which Paul Barrett was on the verge of achieving!

'A fire?' said Tamsyn. 'I didn't know anything about a fire. Did your mum mention it, Josh?'

Josh shook his head.

Tamsyn flipped excitedly back to the long list her search had produced. 'I wonder if there's anything more about it in this lot?'

'Try number seventy-four,' suggested Rob. 'If they're in date order, that's probably the oldest.'

Tamsyn clicked on the final item – only to be shown, to her disappointment, a list of results in the Abbey School swimming gala from five years previously.

'And that's the oldest on the Net?' she cried. 'Five years? Come on!'

'Seems reasonable,' said a familiar voice from behind them. They all swung round to see Mr Findlay, watching them. They'd been concentrating so hard they hadn't heard him come into the room – or the visitor standing next to him.

'Any of you see *why* it's reasonable?' said the teacher.

It was Rob who answered. 'You can only get off the Net what somebody's put on it. And there's nothing more than five years old on-line about Abbey School.'

'What were you trying to do?' asked the man standing next to Mr Findlay.

The three friends swung round to look at him. He was wearing an expensive suit. A gold watch shone from one wrist, an identity bracelet from the other.

'We got a bit sidetracked,' said Rob. 'We're trying to gather information for a possible Abbey site on the Net.'

'Stuff about ex-Abbeyites and where they are now,' chipped in Josh. 'E-mail addresses especially.'

'Then you can start with me,' said the man with a smiling glance at Mr Findlay.

The teacher introduced him. 'This is Councillor Barrett ...'

'Councillor Barrett?' said Rob at once. 'The guy – I mean, the person – who'll be opening the Tech. Block extension?'

Barrett nodded, looking pleased with himself. 'The very guy – I mean, person,' he said. 'In fact, that's why I'm here. I thought I'd better go over my speech with Mr Findlay, just to make sure I wasn't planning to say anything that would embarrass him.'

He took two typewritten sheets from his inside jacket pocket and unfolded them. 'There you are. Just the two pages. Spread the word. Councillor Barrett's speech may be boring, but it won't be long!'

'We've just been reading about the opening of the Tech. Block,' said Tamsyn. 'In today's *Chronicle* ...'

'Today's edition?' said Barrett. 'I *am* impressed. I haven't seen that myself, yet. What does it say? Nothing bad, I hope.'

'It says you were here twenty-five years ago,' said Josh. 'So ...' he added as the thought struck him, '… you must have been in the same year as my mum!'

'Really? What's her name?' said Barrett.

'Tina …' began Josh. He was about to use his surname, then realized that his mum wouldn't have been 'Allan' then – not until she'd married. 'Tina Kerrens,' he said. 'That was her name, then.'

Barrett nodded. 'Tina Kerrens. Yes, of course I remember her. Do you know, I haven't seen her since I left. What's her married name?'

'Allan,' said Josh. 'She married Geoff Allan. He went to Maylands.'

'Councillor Barrett is one of our most distinguished ex-pupils,' Mr Findlay said. 'In fact, there's a very good chance that he will become our next Lord Mayor.'

'Pretty certain, actually,' said Barrett with a satisfied smile. 'I hear from the other councillors it should all be plain sailing. The election at our meeting in May is merely a formality.'

'There you are, Josh. How about that for an item on your Net page?'

'Not forgetting my e-mail ID,' said Barrett, 'It's BARRETT@SYSCO.CO.UK – SysCo's the name of my company. You may have noticed my HQ. New building in Northern Parade. I have a few smaller places dotted around the planet.'

Modest with it! thought Rob. But a contact was a contact, and their project had to start somewhere. 'Do you know any other past pupils who are on the Net, Mr Barrett?'

He thought briefly, then shook his head. 'Sorry. When you're globe-trotting like I've been you lose contact with people pretty quickly. I can hardly remember anyone who was in my year.'

'Except for Tina Kerrens,' said Josh.

'Of course,' said Paul Barrett, turning to Josh. 'Tell you what. If I do come up with anything, I'll send it on. What's your e-mail address, Josh?'

'ALLSTAR@ABBEY.PRIME.CO.UK,' he replied.

'Hang on, let me write that down,' said Barrett. 'I've got a terrible memory.' He quickly wrote down Josh's e-mail address on the back of his speech, then tucked the pages back into his inside pocket. 'OK, anything I remember, I'll be in touch.'

'Can you include the fire in that, please?' asked Tamsyn.

'Fire?'

'Yes. We might want to put in a few bits of school history as well and the piece in the on-line *Chronicle* says there was a fire here in your time.'

The two men exchanged glances. It was Paul Barrett who spoke first, shaking his head as he did so. 'It caused a lot of disruption around exam time, young lady. That's about all I can remember, I'm afraid.'

'But can you think ...'

'The fire was a long time ago,' Mr Findlay cut in.

Barrett smiled. 'I should have been gone a long time ago, too. Pressure of business and all that. Sorry, Jack.'

'Of course,' said Mr Findlay, ushering him

towards the door. 'Good of you to come in to see how the extension is progressing.

'It's very impressive,' he said. And then, pausing only to offer a 'Nice to meet you all' to Tamsyn, Rob and Josh, he followed Mr Findlay down the corridor.

They all looked at each other. 'Well, what sort of message did you think *they* were sending?' said Tamsyn.

'About the fire?' said Rob. 'Keep off, I'd say.'

'So what are we going to do?' asked Tamsyn.

'Obvious,' said Josh, surprising Tamsyn and Rob with the firm edge to his voice. 'We carry on investigating.'

And he'd do it on his own if necessary, thought Josh. Because for the second time in two days he felt as though he'd been talking to somebody who had something to hide.

CHAPTER 3

Abbey School. 12.48 p.m.

'So, how are we going to go about it?' said Tamsyn when they met up in the school library at lunchtime.

'Let's split up the work,' said Rob. 'How about if I look at how we can contact any ex-Abbeyites over the Net?'

Tamsyn nodded. 'OK. And I'll get in touch with the reporter who wrote that piece in the *Chronicle*.' She checked the name she'd written down that morning. 'Debbie Grant.'

'How? We're supposed to be using the Net, remember.'

'No problem. I'll send her a press release by e-mail! I'll check out the on-line *Chronicle* and find her address.'

'How about if I take care of that?' said Josh. 'Sounds like there'll be a lot of typing going on, and I'm the quickest on the keyboard. I can set up a simple database as well, and put anything we find out straight into it.'

Tamsyn and Rob agreed readily. Josh was like lightning on the keyboard.

'Type on, Josh!' said Tamsyn. 'You'll have my press release in your sticky hands by the end of the day!'

5.20 p.m.
Josh pushed his chair back, locked his fingers and stretched his arms. It had been some typing session.

Tamsyn had been as good as her word. No sooner had the bell gone for the end of school than she'd thrust two closely-written pages under his nose. How she'd managed to do it *and* come up with sensible answers to the English questions Ms Gillies had been firing out all afternoon he did not know, but manage she had. Josh had typed it up in the form of an e-mail.

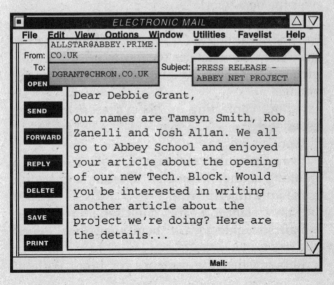

ELECTRONIC MAIL

File Edit View Options Window Utilities Favelist Help

From: ALLSTAR@ABBEY.PRIME.CO.UK
To: DGRANT@CHRON.CO.UK

Subject: PRESS RELEASE – ABBEY NET PROJECT

OPEN
SEND
FORWARD
REPLY
DELETE
SAVE
PRINT

Dear Debbie Grant,

Our names are Tamsyn Smith, Rob Zanelli and Josh Allan. We all go to Abbey School and enjoyed your article about the opening of our new Tech. Block. Would you be interested in writing another article about the project we're doing? Here are the details...

Mail:

Tamsyn had explained in detail about the school's use of the Net and about their plans for an Abbey School site. She had asked for ex-Abbeyite *Chronicle* readers on the Net to contact them.

Finally, almost as if it were an afterthought, Tamsyn had cleverly asked a question.

```
p.s. Your article mentioned a fire that
occurred at Abbey School 25 years ago.
Is there any way of finding out more
about it?
```

As Josh hit SEND to fire the note on its way, Rob arrived. He'd arranged for Mrs Zanelli to pick him up later than usual so that he could spend some time in the library polishing off some overdue homework.

'Finished early!' he said as he pushed through the door. 'I thought I'd flip through the Internet manual in the reference section, to see if it would give me any ideas. And guess what – it gave me an idea!'

'About contacting ex-Abbeyites on the Net?' asked Josh.

'Spot on.'

Josh gave him a quizzical look. He'd been thinking about the problem himself, and hadn't come up with an answer.

'This I want to hear! I don't see how can you e-mail someone to ask them what their e-mail address is …'

Rob finished the sentence for him. 'Without

knowing what their e-mail address is in the first place – right?'

'Right.'

'What about mailing lists?' said Rob, powering up one of the other computers.'

Of course! realized Josh. On the Net there were hundreds of mailing lists – groups of Net users who were interested in the same topics. But … surely there was still a problem?

'Come on,' he said. 'You're not expecting to find a mailing list of past Abbey pupils.

Rob shook his head. 'Nah. But there might be one that'll give us a flying start.' He took a notepad from his bag. 'Now, assuming the manual's right, all we have to do is send an e-mail to a MAILSERV computer – standing for mailing list server, I suppose.'

Josh went into e-mail and typed in what Rob had written down.

```
MAILSERV ALL
```

'And that's it?' said Josh, after clicking on the SEND button. 'What's it going to do?'

'According to the manual, give us a big list of mailing lists that the MAILSERV system manages.'

A sudden bip from their PC was followed by a change in the status line to read MAIL: 1 ITEM WAITING. 'Sounds like that could be it already,' said Rob.

Josh opened the reply – and his mouth fell open as he read the first lines.

```
Your request processed.
There follows details of ALL mailing lists
serviced by MAILSERV.
As of today, this number stands at 4012
mailing lists.
```

'Four thousand and twelve! We'll be here for ever! Come on, man, there must be a way of narrowing it down.'

Rob looked at his notes. He'd only written down that one way. But …

'Maybe the ALL is a sort of search parameter?' he murmured.

'And we can switch it for something else?' said Josh. 'What about "Portsmouth"?'

Rob nodded. 'I reckon that'll get us near enough.'

'So let's go for it,' said Josh. He tried again, this time putting MAILSERV PORTSMOUTH.

```
Your request processed.
There follows details of mailing lists
serviced by MAILSERV with PORTSMOUTH in
their description.
As of today, this number stands at 4
mailing lists.
```

'Better!' said Josh when the reply came back a minute later. 'Much better. Only four instead of four thousand!' He checked them out.

```
AHOY THERE! - Old comrades mailing list
for those who were based in Portsmouth,
England during World War II. Contact:
MAILSERV-AHOY@CENTRE.EDUCOM.EDU
```

```
PORT HISTORY - For those interested in the
history of major world ports, e.g. Odessa,
Boston, Portsmouth etc. Contact:
MAILSERV-PORTHIST@CENTRE.EDUCOM.EDU

TWIN TOWNS - Mailing list of on-line
residents of twin towns Le Havre, France
and Portsmouth, Virginia, USA. Contact:
MAILSERV-TWIN@CENTRE.EDUCOM.EDU

POMPEY PEOPLE - Stay in touch! A mailing
list for people who used to live in
Portsmouth, England. Contact:
MAILSERV-POMPEY@CENTRE.EDUCOM.EDU
```

'Jackpot!' said Josh, pointing eagerly at the
fourth on the list.

'Excellent,' agreed Rob, heading for the door.
'Now all you have to do is e-mail the mailing list
asking anybody who used to come here to get in
touch.'

'All *I* have to do?' said Josh.

'You did offer to type, Josh!' Rob said, looking
at his watch. 'And, as much as I'd love to help,
my driver will be waiting at the gates for me!'

When Rob had gone, Josh composed the note,
repeating much of what Tamsyn's press release
had said, and fired it off to the POMPEY PEOPLE
mailing list.

Finally he sent copies to Lauren, Mitch and
Tom, with a brief explanation of what they were
up to.

It had been a lot of work. Would they have
anything to show for it?

Offices of the Portsmouth Chronicle.
Wednesday 3rd April, 4.10 p.m.

Tamsyn pushed through the revolving doors and into the reception area. The reply from Debbie Grant had been waiting for them that morning.

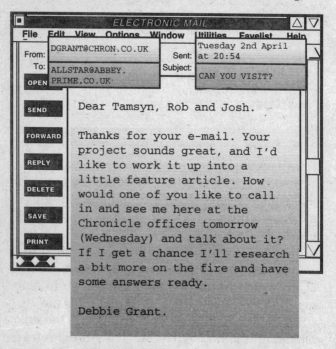

'I thought you said you were going to settle down with old Charlie Dickens and finish off *Great Expectations*.' Rob and Josh had teased Tamsyn before agreeing that, as she'd written the press release in the first place, she actually deserved to be the one to go.

Tamsyn sat down on a soft chair to wait. For a couple of minutes she watched the exciting bustle of photographers carrying equipment and couriers delivering packages, until a smart young woman came hurrying through a side door towards her.

'Tamsyn? Hi, I'm Debbie Grant. Pleased to meet you. Follow me and we'll talk.'

The journalist led the way up to a vast open-plan office on the first floor.

'Big, isn't it?' said Tamsyn to herself.

'This is my corner,' smiled Debbie, pointing Tamsyn towards a desk cluttered with papers. In the centre was a PC.

'Are you on the Net?' asked Tamsyn, then almost kicked herself. 'Of course you are, how could we have e-mailed you otherwise!'

Debbie Grant pulled up a chair for Tamsyn, then sat down at the keyboard. 'We have our own internal network, too. Look, I'll show you.' She pointed at the screen. 'See anything familiar?'

Tamsyn nodded. Almost jumping out at her from the screen was a headline:

INTERNET INVESTIGATORS

Abbey School Pupils in World-Wide Search

'This is the article I've written based on what you sent me,' said Debbie Grant. She scrolled through it, giving Tamsyn time to read what she'd written.

'From here,' she went on, 'I send it to my sub-editor, Colin McGilray. All the other local news journalists do the same. Colin then has to arrange everything so that it fits into the number of pages he's got.'

Tamsyn frowned. 'What if there's not enough room in the newspaper?'

Debbie drew a hand across her throat and smiled. 'Then something gets chopped! It may only be a few sentences – or half the article if things are really tight!'

'I hope that's not going to happen to this one.'

'Me, too,' said Debbie Grant. She smiled. 'But we should be OK. Colin McGilray used to go to the Abbey himself.'

Tamsyn laughed. 'So long as he enjoyed it there! What happens to your article after the sub-editor's done with it?' she asked.

'When all the sub-editors have completed their pages, the final stage is to compile them into a large file for printing. That's pretty much the same file you're looking at when you surf the Net for the on-line version of the *Chronicle*.'

Tamsyn turned back to the screen. The final few sentences of Debbie Grant's article were showing.

So come on, you surfers. If you're ex-Abbey and on-line, send an e-mail to:
ALLSTAR@ABBEY.PRIME.CO.UK

They want to know where you are now, what you're doing, anything you can remember about life at the Abbey ... teachers, classrooms, old friends, school blazers. (And don't forget the school blaze 25 years ago!) Come on, if you've got any information at all they're waiting for you to 'fire' them a note with the details!

'Sorry about the rotten jokes at the end,' said Debbie. She looked serious for a moment. 'Maybe it'll do the trick, though. Because I'm afraid I can't help you much on that side of things. I checked right through our microfiche archives about that fire and, do you know, there was hardly anything on it.'

'No?' said Tamsyn, surprised.

'No,' said Debbie. 'The bare facts were reported and that was it. One classroom was completely gutted, but the firefighters got there in time to stop it spreading to the whole school.'

'And that's all?'

'There was a bit more. Not on the fire specifically. But a couple of days later there was a report about a boy being expelled. Permanently Excluded, I think they call it nowadays.'

'Did it say who?' asked Tamsyn.

'No. Maybe the name wasn't released.'

'And you think ...'

'That the mystery boy started the fire?' Debbie Grant nodded. 'Two and two makes four, wouldn't you say?'

CHAPTER 4

Abbey School.
Thursday 4th April, 8.25 a.m.

On her way to school, Tamsyn bought a copy of that day's edition of the *Portsmouth Chronicle*. From the small newsagent's at the bottom of the road she broke into a run, and didn't stop until she met up with Rob and Josh at the school gates. Dropping her bag onto the ground, she begin to riffle urgently through the tabloid pages.

'The article,' she puffed. 'Debbie Grant said it'd be in this edition.'

'No!' grinned Rob. 'And there I was, thinking you were checking for your horoscope!'

'What's the matter with the on-line version?' said Josh. 'That's free. You could have saved yourself some money.'

Tamsyn continued turning the pages. 'Josh, there are some things a computer screen can't replace – and the lovely *feel* of a newspaper is one of them!'

Her eyes roamed over the page she'd reached. 'Here it is! It's in!'

As Josh looked over her shoulder, Tamsyn

crouched down so that Rob could read Debbie Grant's article as well.

'It's all here, just as I saw it on her system at the offices,' said Tamsyn. 'Every bit of—'

She stopped as she read the final paragraph.

'Problem?' said Josh, looking at her.

Tamsyn looked again at the end of Debbie Grant's article.

So come on, you surfers. If you're ex-Abbey and on-line, send an e-mail to:

ALLSTAR@ABBEY.PRIME.CO.UK

They want to know where you are now, what you're doing, anything you can remember about life at the Abbey ... teachers, classrooms, old friends, school blazers – anything. Come on, they're waiting for you to send them a note with the details!

'It's been cut. There was a bit about the fire at the end. And the last sentence had a grotty joke in it.'

'Maybe that's *why* it was cut,' said Rob.

'Maybe,' said Tamsyn. 'She did say that her sub-editor might have to chop it down if there wasn't enough room.'

Josh pointed down at the page. At the bottom of the article there was a clear gap. 'But there *was* enough room,' he said.

**Perth, Australia. Thursday 4th April,
7.40 p.m. (UK time, 11.40 a.m.)**

'Wow!' said Tom.

There was a CRIME section on the Net – and,
within that, a section on fingerprinting.

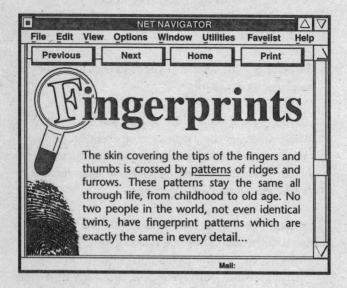

Tom saw that the first appearance of the word
'patterns' was underlined. This, he knew, indicat-
ed a hypertext link to some further information.
Moving the mouse over the word, he clicked. At
once, a new screen appeared.

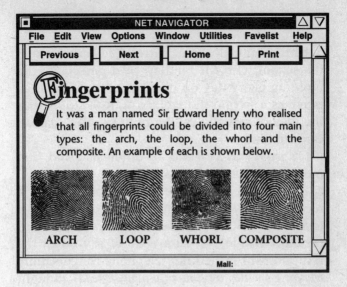

NET NAVIGATOR

File   Edit   View   Options   Window   Utilities   Favelist   Help

Previous   Next   Home   Print

Fingerprints

It was a man named Sir Edward Henry who realised that all fingerprints could be divided into four main types: the arch, the loop, the whorl and the composite. An example of each is shown below.

ARCH   LOOP   WHORL   COMPOSITE

Mail:

Tom read on, fascinated, until the clank of a cleaning bucket from the corridor outside told him that his mum had finished her evening's work. *Having a school cleaner for a mum is a definite bonus!* thought Tom. He hit the PRINT button and saw the lights on the front of the laser printer begin to flash. Moments later, sheets of paper were streaming out.

Peterson's Prints Principle was making progress!

SysCo House, Portsmouth.
Thursday 4th April, 3.40 p.m.
It was the large triangular *SysCo House* sign, mounted high above the shimmering glass

entrance for the world to see, that gave Josh the idea.

Until Councillor Paul Barrett had turned up at the school with Mr Findlay, he'd passed by the building every day on his way home without so much as a second thought. Now, Josh stopped as the idea of actually calling in to see Paul Barrett came to him.

OK, so it was a bit cheeky. But he had said, 'Let me know if I can help in any way' …

He walked up to the glass doors. Inside, a receptionist was busy answering the telephone. Josh pushed through the doors and stood uncertainly inside, not sure what to say when the receptionist finished her telephone conversation. *Maybe I should fire him an e-mail instead?* thought Josh. Yes, that's what he would do.

And then, as he was about to turn away, Paul Barrett himself came out through an office door and saw him. The businessman frowned then, recognizing Josh, gave him a welcoming smile. Before he knew it, Josh had been ushered into Paul Barrett's plush office and was sinking into one of his soft leather chairs.

'Josh, isn't it? Nice to see you again.' Barrett perched himself on the corner of the largest desk Josh had ever seen. 'How's the project going?'

'OK, thanks,' said Josh. 'We've found a mailing list that might have some good contacts.'

'Really? What's that?'

'Pompey People,' said Josh. 'People who used

to live in Portsmouth and have moved away. Apparently quite a few of them still keep in touch with what's happening in the City. With a bit of luck there'll be some ex-Abbeyites on there.'

'You've e-mailed the list, have you?'

'Yeah,' said Josh. 'Told them what we're up to.'

'Any replies yet?'

'No,' said Josh. 'It's early days, but we haven't got much time. That's why I called in. To see if you've come up with any?'

Barrett shook his head slowly. 'Nothing, I'm afraid. Not that you should have held out any hope with me. I've got a memory like a leaky bucket,' he added with a broad smile.

Josh glanced around the room. Beside Paul Barrett's massive desk was a low table littered with business journals and magazines. Lying on top of the pile was a copy of a newspaper he recognized.

'Tamsyn met a journalist and had a piece put in the *Chronicle*,' said Josh. 'Did you see it?'

Barrett picked up the newspaper, but didn't open it. 'Yes. Very good, wasn't it?'

'There was a bit missing.' The words were out before Josh knew it.

'Missing?'

'Well, cut. A bit on the end.'

'Editors can do that, Josh. They're a law unto themselves.'

'It was a bit asking if anybody could tell us more about the fire.'

Councillor Barrett looked a little surprised.

'Well … we found out a bit more about it, you see,' Josh continued.

'More about it?'

Josh nodded. Recalling what Tamsyn had told them that morning, he said, 'Somebody got expelled because of it, didn't they?'

'Josh,' said Barrett slowly. 'Look, take my advice. Forget the fire.'

'Why?' said Josh, feeling a jab of irritation.

With a sigh, Barrett eased himself off the corner of his desk and sat down behind it. Looking straight at Josh, he said. 'You said your mum is Tina Kerrens as was, right? And she married Geoff Allan.'

Josh nodded, not seeing what this had to do with anything. 'Yeah, like I said. My mum was in your year.'

'They were both in my year, Josh.'

'No, you're wrong. They couldn't have been. Not both of them. I told you, Dad went to Maylands.'

Even as Josh was speaking, Barrett began to shake his head. 'I'm sorry, Josh, *you're* the one who's wrong. Geoff was in my year, too. He only went to Maylands after …'

Josh felt his stomach tighten. 'After what?'

'After he got expelled from Abbey,' said Paul Barrett. 'I'm sorry to be the one to tell you this, Josh. But … the fire. Geoff Allan started it. Your dad started it.'

* * *

Josh's house. 4.45 p.m.

Josh arrived home in a daze. Had he been right? Had his dad been lying to him – because he hadn't wanted him to find out that he'd been the one who started that fire?

A sick feeling entered Josh's stomach. Surely, *that* couldn't be true? Councillor Barrett had got it wrong, he must have. But – the face in the school photograph. Hadn't he thought when he saw it that it looked like his dad? Hadn't he thought that neither he nor his mum were being straight with him?

It was only when he spotted the note from his mum on the kitchen table that Josh realized the house was empty. She'd had to go out and wouldn't be back until five-thirty.

He slumped into a chair … then got to his feet again. He had to have another look at that photograph.

Hurrying upstairs, he went into his parents' room. The bulging cardboard box had been put away. He found it in a corner and laid it on the bed. He lifted the lid. The rolled-up photograph was on the top. He took it out and stared at that face, the face he'd recognized because it looked so much like his own.

'OK. I admit it. I went to the Abbey.'

The sound of his dad's voice nearly made Josh cry out. So engrossed had he been in the photograph, that Mr Allan had let himself in the front door and come up the stairs without Josh realizing it.

Mr Allan sat beside him. 'I got kicked out, Josh. That's when I went to Maylands.'

Josh looked at him. 'I know.' He took a deep breath. 'I know about the fire, as well.'

For a few seconds, Mr Allan didn't speak. 'Who told you?' he asked finally.

'Councillor Barrett. I was asking him about it today.'

'Paul Barrett,' said Josh's dad, quietly. 'Maybe if I'd been a bit more like him, none of it would have happened.'

'How d'you mean?'

'Oh, just that Barrett knew what he wanted. At that age, I didn't. I just played the fool.' Mr Allan looked steadily at Josh. 'Did he tell you the whole story?'

'Only that you got expelled for starting the fire?'

'He didn't mention the fact that I denied it, then? That I told them all along, it wasn't me.'

Josh looked into his dad's eyes. 'Then it wasn't you?'

'No, it wasn't. But nobody believed me.'

Mr Allan sighed. 'I should have told you all this a long time ago, I suppose. There just wasn't a right time.'

'Now looks like the right time to me, Dad,' said Josh quietly.

Mr Allan smiled, then nodded. 'Reckon so.' He took a deep breath. 'OK. The first thing you have to know is that I was a dumb-head when I was a kid. I didn't see the point of school, found it boring. I was always messing about. Maybe that's partly why I didn't want to tell you – you're getting on so well at the Abbey, I didn't want to give you any daft ideas.'

'So, the fire – what happened?' said Josh quietly.

'Well, that day I had a row with Findlay. Ironic really, because his electronics stuff was the one subject I stayed awake for. He taught us bits about radios and televisions and alarm systems, see? That made it different from history and the rest. I gave him a hard time at first, but when I saw what he was teaching us was actually *useful*, I started listening.'

'You said you had a row,' said Josh.

Mr Allan nodded. 'Yeah. Right at the end of the week it was. We had a double period, either side of Friday afternoon break. We'd all gone out after the first half. When we got back, the soldering iron in my place was red hot and off its stand. It had burnt a hole in the bench. Findlay saw it, assumed I'd been playing the fool again, and went bananas. But I hadn't left that iron on. For once, I was innocent. So …' Mr Allan shrugged, and even blushed, '… I gave him a mouthful.'

Josh smiled at the thought of his dad – who seemed to have spent all Josh's life banging on about being polite – giving Mr Findlay a hard time.

'So what did he do?'

'Threw me out, of course. Sent me to the Head and I got yet another detention. By the time I got home that night I was steamed up good and proper.

'So,' Mr Allan went on, 'that night, I went back. Don't ask me what I planned to do, because I don't know. I took a pair of pliers with me. I'd had this idea of wrecking his alarm system ...'

'What alarm system?'

'Oh, just a simple one Findlay had set up round the electronics room. More as a demonstration than anything else. When it was on, any door or window being opened would set it off. The control box was right at the back, near the bench I used to sit at. At first I'd put my feet up on it, just to annoy him. Anyway, some of the wires ran outside. I'd just snipped a few, when I saw it.'

'Saw what?'

'That classroom had an outside door, Josh. And it hadn't been closed properly.'

'You mean – Mr Findlay left it open?'

'I don't know. Maybe after arguing with me, he'd forgotten to lock up. Anyway, I went in. It was stupid, I know, but I wasn't thinking straight. I went through the classroom and out along the corridor. Then I heard footsteps – two people coming from round the corner, near the Head's study.'

'Burglars?' said Josh. 'Didn't you run for it?'

'I couldn't, I'd gone too far down the corridor. They were between me and the way I'd come in. I did the only thing I could do – dived across to the cloakrooms and shut myself in there. Josh, I was scared. On top of that, just after I heard the footsteps go by I heard the sound of a police car. That just about topped it off! I stayed in that cloakroom for a good quarter of an hour before I came out. That's when I smelt the smoke.'

'Coming from the electronics classroom?' asked Josh.

'Yeah. I raced down there. Somehow the curtains at the back, near where I usually sat, were alight. And the ceiling. It was a temporary classroom, mostly made out of plywood.'

'What did you do?'

Mr Allan shook his head. 'I panicked. Freaked out, I suppose you'd say. I put my jacket over my head and raced through the smoke. And then what? I discovered the door was locked. Whoever they were, they'd locked that door behind them.'

'How'd you get out then?'

'The only way I could. I put my jacket round my sleeve to protect myself, and smashed a window. Then I jumped out and ran for it. I didn't stop till – well, remember the police car I'd heard?'

'While you were hiding? Yes,' nodded Josh.

'It'd actually been called to a traffic accident half a mile away. They were on their way back when I flagged them down. They called the fire brigade. It didn't occur to me for a second that I'd end up being accused of starting the thing.'

'So why did you? How d'you get the blame?'

'Josh, that classroom was ruined but there was

still enough evidence left to prove I'd been there. My jacket, for a start. I'd dropped it before jumping through the window. Then there was the plastic covering round the alarm wires. That had melted, but it was obvious they'd been cut through – and I'd done that. The pliers were still in my pocket!'

'But you didn't start that fire, Dad! It must have been done by whoever else was in the school. Those burglars.'

Josh's dad smiled. 'That's how I worked it out, son. Trouble was, I couldn't prove a thing.'

'Didn't you tell them about the unlocked door?'

'Of course I did.'

'And they didn't believe you?'

Mr Allan shook his head. 'Mr Findlay insisted he'd locked that door straight after our lesson.'

'He could have been wrong.'

'No, I'm sure he did. You see, Josh, the burglars idea didn't hold water. When they searched the school afterwards, nothing had been stolen. There was only one thing missing – and that pointed at me.'

'What? What was it?'

'The key to that door. Mr Findlay's desk was recovered after the fire. The key wasn't there.' Mr Allan shrugged. 'And as the only person who'd definitely been *in* the school, I was the obvious suspect.'

'But you didn't take it!' said Josh. 'Didn't you have any idea who it could have been?

How many kids knew where it was?'

'Every one of us. Half the time it wasn't even in the drawer. Mr Findlay was terrible about leaving his keys lying around.'

'Not any more,' said Josh. 'He's got a clip on his belt now.'

'Maybe that's why,' said Mr Allan. 'Anyway, somebody took it and used it to get in. But it wasn't me.'

'And nobody believed that?'

'Well, let's just say nobody else owned up. And with the evidence against me – well, my feet didn't touch the ground. I was expelled.'

'Couldn't you have ...' Josh was feeling angrier by the second, '... I don't know, couldn't you have done *something*?'

'Not really. Everybody agreed to call it an accident, and keep it out of the papers as much as they could. The insurance money paid for all the damage. In return, it was made pretty obvious that I was expected to go quietly. So I did – to Maylands, where I had to repeat the year.'

Mr Allan got to his feet. 'So, now you know it all.'

'But – you were innocent!' cried Josh, tears pricking his eyes.

Mr Allan ruffled Josh's hair. 'Sometimes it's not much help being innocent if you can't prove it,' he said. 'Anyway, it all worked out. I came to my senses when I got to Maylands. I started working, and went on to night school when I left. Now look at me – running my own business.'

'Mending televisions and the like?' said Josh. 'If it hadn't been for what happened, maybe you could have been up in Councillor Barrett's league.'

'Josh, I wouldn't have wanted to be in Paul Barrett's league. I'm very happy doing what I do.' He bent low to look into Josh's eyes. 'It would just have been nice to have proved I wasn't the one who started that fire. But I'll never be able to do that, and it took until now for me to realize it. I'm sorry I didn't come clean about it to you before. Forgive me?'

Josh nodded. 'Natch.'

As his dad went off downstairs again, Josh looked once more at the old photograph, with its sea of faces. *Was it one of you who really did it?* wondered Josh. It had to be someone who was there at the time, somebody who could have stolen that key. But who? Was it possible to find out?

He didn't know. He simply knew that never in his whole life had he felt so determined to do *something*.

CHAPTER 5

Abbey School. Friday 5th April, 8.35 a.m.

Tamsyn looked at the old leavers' list. 'But where would we start?' she said as Josh finished telling them his dad's story. She tapped at the names on the list. 'We don't even know if it was one of these.'

Nicola ACTON	Niall HARRISON	Connie PASQUALE
Vanessa ARNOLD	Mark HUGHES	Maureen PORTER
Paul BARRETT	Bob JEFFREYS	Ben QUINNLAN
Sophie BRYANT	Mary JONES	Peter SIMONS
Quentin BURWOOD	Tina KERRENS	Rodney SIMPSON
Catherine COLE	Mark KINDER	Michael STARK
Joan COX	Vince LANGFORD	Janice THORPE
Maria DAWSON	Anne LEWIS	Mary VINCENT
Gordon EARLY	Colin McGILRAY	David WILLIAMS
Lucy FISHER	Rhoda MacLEAN	
Alice FROST	Tony NORRIS	

'Surely if there *was* any evidence to prove your dad didn't start that fire,' said Rob, 'it would have disappeared years ago?'

Josh fell silent. They were right. It did seem an impossible task. He just didn't want to admit it.

'I reckon your best hope,' said Tamsyn, though not very confidently, 'is in getting some good replies from the Net. Why don't we check out the e-mail?'

Josh shrugged and logged in. 'Suppose so.'

'Hey!' he cried, suddenly brighter. 'We've got some!' On the status line was the message MAIL: 6 ITEMS WAITING.

They looked at them quickly. The first two were from local recent ex-pupils who'd seen the article in the *Chronicle* and had replied with their e-mail addresses.

'Nothing about the fire, of course,' said Josh. 'If only that bit hadn't been cut.' He opened the third.

'From Japan!' said Rob as he saw the header.

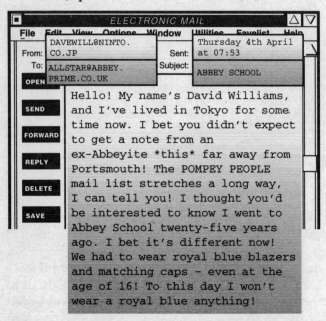

```
┌─────────────────────────────────────────────────┐
│ □        ELECTRONIC MAIL            △ ▽          │
│ File  Edit  View  Options  Window  Utilities  Favelist  Help │
│       ┌──────────────────┐    ┌──────────────────┐│
│ From: │ DAVEWILL@NINTO.  │    │ Thursday 4th April│
│       │ CO.JP            │Sent:│ at 07:53          ││
│ To:   │ ALLSTAR@ABBEY.   │Subject:│                │
│ OPEN  │ PRIME.CO.UK      │    │ ABBEY SCHOOL      ││
│       └──────────────────┘    └──────────────────┘│
│ SEND     Hello! My name's David Williams,         │
│          and I've lived in Tokyo for some         │
│          time now. I bet you didn't expect        │
│ FORWARD  to get a note from an                    │
│          ex-Abbeyite *this* far away from         │
│ REPLY    Portsmouth! The POMPEY PEOPLE            │
│          mail list stretches a long way,          │
│ DELETE   I can tell you! I thought you'd          │
│          be interested to know I went to          │
│ SAVE     Abbey School twenty-five years           │
│          ago. I bet it's different now!           │
│          We had to wear royal blue blazers        │
│          and matching caps - even at the          │
│          age of 16! To this day I won't           │
│          wear a royal blue anything!              │
└─────────────────────────────────────────────────┘
```

> You wanted to know something
> about the fire. That happened
> in my time, though I'm not sure
> I can tell you much. They said
> a boy named Geoff Allan started
> it. I was amazed when I heard.
> He never struck me as the sort
> who'd do something like that.

Rob and Tamsyn looked at Josh. 'That's another one on your side,' said Tamsyn.

'Not proof though, is it?' said Josh. He continued reading the note.

> I can still smell the smoke in
> the air. Evil! Maybe that's why
> I made such a mess of the
> Scholarship exams three of us
> took that week, eh? We were
> supposed to be the top brains in
> the school, but I've never taken
> such a tough exam in my life.
> The other two did pass, and I
> was amazed at Barrett's 96%.
> Anyhow, I'm afraid I can't help
> you much in the way of Net
> addresses. The only one I know
> is in Portsmouth, and you've
> probably got that. It's
> MCGILRAY@CHRON.CO.UK – Colin
> McGilray. He's a sub-editor with
> the Portsmouth Chronicle. I send
> him news snippets from Japan.
>
> All the best – David

SEND

FORWARD

REPLY

DELETE

SAVE

PRINT

Mail:

Josh looked at Tamsyn. 'What did you say the name of Debbie Grant's sub-editor was – the guy who cut the article?'

'McGilray,' said Tamsyn slowly. 'Colin McGilray.'

Rob tapped at Josh's class list. 'It's the same one.'

'The one who cut the bit about the fire?'

'Come on, Josh,' said Rob at once, 'you're not saying he cut it on purpose? Why would he do that?'

'To stop us finding out more?' shrugged Josh, then added at once, 'OK, don't say it – pretty unlikely, huh?' He clicked through the remaining three messages. Two were from recent leavers and they didn't even mention the fire.

He opened the final note, and his heart jumped. 'Look at this one!'

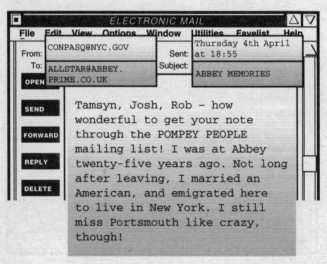

ELECTRONIC MAIL

File Edit View Options Window Utilities Favelist Help

From: CONPASQ@NYC.GOV
To: ALLSTAR@ABBEY.PRIME.CO.UK
Sent: Thursday 4th April at 18:55
Subject: ABBEY MEMORIES

OPEN SEND FORWARD REPLY DELETE

Tamsyn, Josh, Rob – how wonderful to get your note through the POMPEY PEOPLE mailing list! I was at Abbey twenty-five years ago. Not long after leaving, I married an American, and emigrated here to live in New York. I still miss Portsmouth like crazy, though!

As for memories of the Abbey, I
could write you a whole book
about my time there! We had to
pack an extra trunk just to
bring out my stack of
memorabilia! If only you could
jump on a plane and fly over
here, you could see it all!
Look, I haven't got much time
right now. I just wanted to
touch base with you, and
let you know I'll be mailing
you again soon.
Cheers, Connie Pasquale.

FORWARD

REPLY

DELETE

SAVE

PRINT

Mail:

The three friends looked at each other. New
York? New York meant Mitch! Maybe he could
help out on this one.

By the time the bell went for registration,
Connie Pasquale's note had been fired across to
Mitch.

'Nine a.m. here, four a.m. in New York,' said
Josh. 'Mitch'll see that the minute he gets to work!'

New York, USA.
7.40 a.m. (UK time: 12.40 p.m.)
Mitch saw Connie Pasquale's e-mail, forwarded
from Portsmouth, before he started work.

He decided to check out her User ID in the
Net's New York on-line directory and find her

home telephone number. His call was answered on the second ring. Mitch explained who he was, and all about his connection with Abbey School in the UK.

'Sure! I can let you see some stuff in person.' Connie Pasquale's voice sounded cheery even at that time in the morning. 'Look, why don't I bring some in with me to work? Could you manage to get over there?' She gave the name of a government building just a couple of blocks away. 'I'm on the ground floor, just ask at Reception. Can you make lunchtime? One o'clock, say?'

'No prob,' said Mitch.

'Get ready for a session, mind,' said the voice at the other end of the line. 'I have got *so much* stuff! Report books, record cards, programmes, pictures, autographs, fingerprints …'

'Fingerprints?' said Mitch.

'Oh, yes! It was my special thing. I didn't just collect everybody's autograph, I got them to give me their thumbprints as well!'

'Sounds wacky,' said Mitch. 'But cool.'

Connie Pasquale laughed. 'It was! Look, Mitch, I'll never get to work at this rate. I'll photocopy some bits and have them ready for you, OK? Bye!'

Mitch put the phone down. It sounded like Josh and Co. had struck lucky!

New York. 12.58 p.m. (UK time: 5.58 p.m.)
Like most government buildings, the one Mitch

had been directed to was dull and grey. A flight of stone steps led up to a panelled front door with a gleaming brass knob. Mitch pushed through it and into an entrance hall. The receptionist's desk was on the far side. He was directed down a grey, plain corridor where he found a door with a nameplate: Connie Pasquale, Manhattan District Environment Officer.

He knocked and went in – just in time to see a plump, blonde-haired woman tipping some papers into the bin at the side of her desk. She looked up, startled.

'Sorry, ma'am. Didn't mean to make you jump,' said Mitch. 'I guess you're Connie Pasquale. I'm Mitch Zanelli. I called this morning.' He took a seat beside the desk.

The woman gave him a nervous smile. *Something's up*, thought Mitch at once. He felt none of the cheeriness that had zoomed down the phone at him that morning.

'Look, Mitch,' she said haltingly. 'I'm afraid I've brought you all the way here for nothing. I ... well, I haven't had time to copy anything.'

No time to copy anything? Mitch glanced at the full trash bin. *So what's that lot?*

'I can come back later,' he said. 'No hassle.'

Connie Pasquale shook her head at the suggestion. 'No. I don't think it's worth it. Anyway, I'm not sure the stuff I've got would be of interest to anybody other than me. It's just a pile of silly memories from long ago.'

'You sounded real sure earlier,' said Mitch.

'I … I've had second thoughts,' said Connie Pasquale, clearly embarrassed. 'I understand there was a boy expelled around my time. For starting a fire. His son goes to Abbey School now. If I tell your friends anything … well, it could cause problems. So – sorry.'

'That's OK,' said Mitch, taking another glance at the trash bin. Some sheets were poking out at an angle, almost within reach. Mitch slowly stretched out a hand …

As Connie Pasquale showed the meeting was over by turning to the computer sitting on a stand behind her, Mitch plucked a page from the bin and slid it inside his folder. She didn't look round as Mitch left.

Manor House. Saturday 6th April, 10.30 a.m.

Tamsyn, with Josh at her side, punched the button above the security panel. A tinny voice rattled out at them.

'Hello?'

'It's Tamsyn and Josh.'

'Who?'

'Oi!' laughed Tamsyn. 'Open up!'

They heard Rob laugh, then a buzzer rasped and the front door clicked open. Tamsyn and Josh stepped inside. Rob was waiting for them at the far end of the hall. 'I'm down here,' he called. 'You caught me mid-surf.'

'Any more replies?' asked Josh at once.

'I wouldn't know,' grinned Rob. 'They're all

coming back to you, remember? Come on, I'll log off and you can log in.'

He moved to one side to let Josh on to the keyboard. Josh went through the log-in sequence, keying in his User ID and password. An e-mail from Mitch was waiting for him, along with a few others.

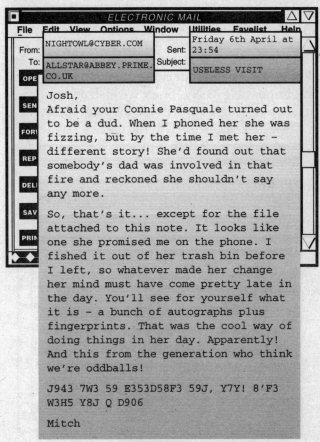

ELECTRONIC MAIL

File   Edit   View   Options   Window   Utilities   Favelist   Help

From: NIGHTOWL@CYBER.COM

To: ALLSTAR@ABBEY.PRIME.CO.UK

Sent: Friday 6th April at 23:54

Subject: USELESS VISIT

Josh,
Afraid your Connie Pasquale turned out to be a dud. When I phoned her she was fizzing, but by the time I met her – different story! She'd found out that somebody's dad was involved in that fire and reckoned she shouldn't say any more.

So, that's it... except for the file attached to this note. It looks like one she promised me on the phone. I fished it out of her trash bin before I left, so whatever made her change her mind must have come pretty late in the day. You'll see for yourself what it is - a bunch of autographs plus fingerprints. That was the cool way of doing things in her day. Apparently! And this from the generation who think we're oddballs!

J943 7W3 59 E353D58F3 59J, Y7Y! 8'F3 W3H5 Y8J Q D906

Mitch

'Found out about my dad?' said Josh. 'How?'

'Somebody told her, that's all it could be,' said Tamsyn.

'But *why*?'

Rob answered. 'To stop you finding out that it was your dad who was expelled for it. I mean, she's not to know you've already found out.'

'OK, then,' said Josh. '*How* did somebody know we were even going to see Connie Pasquale?'

'The Net?' suggested Tamsyn. 'We're trying to find out who's on it. Maybe one of the other ex-Abbeyites we've contacted got in touch with her? It's impossible to say.' She gave Josh an encouraging smile. 'Come on, let's see the fingerprint file.'

Josh clicked on SAVE to file the note away, then pulled in the file Mitch had sent. It looked just as he'd imagined, a jumble of signatures and thumbprints.

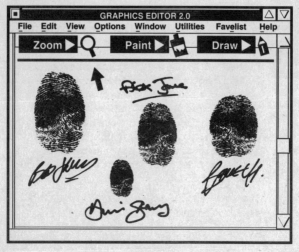

Josh shrugged. *So what?* He had the full list of names already from the class list.

'Good try, Mitch,' he said, clicking on SAVE again before switching back to e-mail.

'There's more,' said Tamsyn, pointing at the bottom of the screen with its MAIL: 3 ITEMS WAITING display. 'Maybe they'll have some better news.'

'Hang on,' said Rob. 'I want to know what the code part says.'

'Is it important?' said Josh, irritated.

'Don't bite my head off, man,' said Rob. 'It might be.'

Impatiently, Josh waited as Rob reversed what Mitch had typed at the bottom of his note.

```
MORE USE TO DETECTIVE TOM, HUH!
I'VE SENT HIM A COPY
```

'Great,' said Josh flatly. 'Now maybe we can look at the rest of this e-mail.'

The first two were a disappointment. They were simply replies from recent ex-pupils, giving their User IDs and little more. Josh opened the third.

'Hey. It's from France!' said Tamsyn.

'And another one from my dad's year,' said Josh.

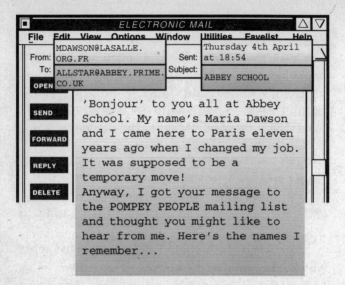

File   Edit   View   Options   Window   Utilities   Favelist   Help

From: MDAWSON@LASALLE.ORG.FR

To: ALLSTAR@ABBEY.PRIME.CO.UK

Sent: Thursday 4th April at 18:54

Subject: ABBEY SCHOOL

OPEN SEND FORWARD REPLY DELETE

'Bonjour' to you all at Abbey
School. My name's Maria Dawson
and I came here to Paris eleven
years ago when I changed my job.
It was supposed to be a
temporary move!
Anyway, I got your message to
the POMPEY PEOPLE mailing list
and thought you might like to
hear from me. Here's the names I
remember...

The note went on to list ten or so names. Once
again, Josh checked them against his list. They all
matched.

As to where they all are now, I
haven't got a clue. I did hear
that Dave Williams moved to
Tokyo a while back. He was my
dreamboat! I remember gazing at
him for an hour while he was
sitting an exam with two other
boys!

That reminds me, I heard that
one of them went abroad too.
Toronto, I think. Quinnell or
Quintin? Q-something, anyway.
Whoever he was, he was into

INTERNET DETECTIVES

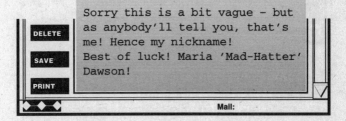

technology (I remember he got
on well with Mr Findlay) so you
could find he's on the Net
somewhere as well.

Sorry this is a bit vague — but
as anybody'll tell you, that's
me! Hence my nickname!
Best of luck! Maria 'Mad-Hatter'
Dawson!

DELETE

SAVE

PRINT

Mail:

'The mysterious "Q-something",' said Rob
with a laugh. He checked the list. 'It must have
been Quentin Burwood or Ben Quinnlan.'

'Or Connie Pasquale,' said Josh dismally. 'We
could be going round in a circle here.'

Tamsyn tapped her fingers on Josh's head.
'Hello! Anyone at home in there? Connie
Pasquale's in New York, not Toronto, and she's a
she not a he!'

'So, Quentin or Quinnlan. Not a lot of help,
then …' Rob suddenly he grinned as an idea
struck him. 'Unless Lauren can track him down
in Toronto, of course!'

'Fat chance,' snapped Josh. 'Get real, eh?'

'Fat chance, maybe,' laughed Tamsyn, trying
to cheer Josh up. 'But that's no reason for not
suggesting it.' She nudged Josh's elbow. 'Go
on, e-mail Lauren. You know how much she
loves a challenge!'

CHAPTER 6

Toronto, Canada. Saturday 6th April, 8.40 a.m. (UK time: 1.40 p.m.)

'Find somebody called Quentin or Quinnlan who might have gone to Abbey school?' cried Lauren when she saw Josh's note. 'In a city the size of Toronto! Fine! No problem! Just give me ten years or so!'

'They say talking to yourself is the first sign of madness,' chuckled a voice from the depths of an armchair in the corner of the small room.

Lauren swung round to face her grandmother, Alice. 'Then you must be completely gone, Allie,' laughed Lauren, 'because you've been nattering to yourself for years!'

The chubby, grey-haired lady laughed again. 'You think I'm mad, eh?' She nodded. 'Yep, you could be right. That's probably why I've decided to take you out this morning and get that skimmer you've been ear-bashing me about for weeks.'

'Really?' cried Lauren. She was so excited she didn't bother to tell Alice it was a scanner not a skimmer. 'Really, really? Yeah!'

She swung back to the keyboard and quickly took herself into the NET NAVIGATOR. Moments later she'd swooped through the levels of menu to reach one in particular.

'On-line shopping, Allie,' said Lauren. 'We can order and pay for one over the Net. It'll be delivered by snail-mail though.'

Alice eased herself out of her chair. 'No, ma'am. Call me old-fashioned, but I like to see what I'm buying before I hand over my money. I haven't forgotten that chess tutor!'

Some months before, Alice had paid for a chess CD-ROM over the Net, only to discover that the boss of the company concerned had run off with her money and that of hundreds of others too.

'We did help catch him, Allie!' said Lauren.

'Maybe, but I can live without that sort of excitement.' She pottered out into the kitchen. 'Hold it, I'll just go get a pen and paper. Find some addresses for me to write down.'

'There's plenty of them, Allie,' called Lauren as she brought up a list which filled the screen. She hit PAGE DOWN to continue the list. 'Dozens of them!'

And then she saw it, down towards the end of the list.

```
PC Partners, Eaton Centre
Phil's Computer Mart, Carlton Street
Quinnlan Computer Systems, Yorke Street
Right Software, Dundas Street West
Systems Solutions, Eaton Centre
X-tatic Computers, Yonge Street
```

'Quinnlan Computer Systems?' she murmured. 'Come on. That just can't be the one Josh is after.'

As Allie clattered on in the kitchen in her search for a pen, Lauren switched out and across to the on-line Toronto Telephone Directory. She moved the cursor up to the top of the screen, to the ever-present SEARCH FOR? panel.

She typed: QUINNLAN.

Within moments, her answer was back. There were just two in the whole of the City. Quinnlan Computer Systems was one. The other was QUINNLAN, L.B. Could that be the one? Lauren saw the addition next to the name: 'Ms'. No way was that going to be *Ben* Quinnlan!

'Found it,' said Allie, pottering back in from the kitchen with a pen in her hand. She settled down at the table. 'Right, shoot!' she said, only to squawk before Lauren could say a word, 'Oh, this dratted pen!'

'Allie, you know that pen leaks,' said Lauren.

Alice was dabbing ink from her fingers. 'And *you* know I hate those ballpoint thingies. This is a real pen, with real ink …'

'Which makes a real mess,' laughed Lauren.

'Only because I forget which way to hold it,' said Allie. She stopped dabbing and prepared to write. 'OK. Where do you want to go?'

Lauren looked at the screen list again. It was more than an Internet Detective could resist.

'Quinnlan Computer Systems,' she said. 'Yorke Street.'

Downtown Toronto.
Saturday 6th April, 10.40 a.m.
'There it is, Allie!'

Quinnlan Computer Systems was a moderately large store, set back from the road and with a parking area in front. Its windows were splashed with 'special offer' adverts. Through them, Lauren could see a number of computer systems, each cycling endlessly through the opening sequences of games.

Allie eased her old car into one of the parking spots. 'You can do the talking,' she said to Lauren.

'You know what sort of skimmer you're after.'

'Scanner, Allie!'

Inside, Lauren headed for the youngest sales assistant she could see. They were led across to a glass cabinet full of different types of hand scanners.

Lauren looked them over, her mind on other things. She'd spent enough time reading magazines and reviews on the Net to know exactly which one she wanted. But simply buying it there and then wasn't going to get her a conversation with Mr Quinnlan. He, presumably, was the boss – and, Lauren assumed, the boss would only come out if there was a problem of some sort.

So, she gave the sales assistant a problem. 'That one,' said Lauren innocently, as she pointed at a neat hand scanner, 'can you tell me if the software that comes with it can handle Optical Character Recognition?'

The assistant looked blank. 'Er … I'm not sure. What was that again? Optical …'

Lauren repeated the question – and got the same blank face from the assistant. 'How about image scaling and merging then?'

It was enough. With a mutter of, 'Hang on. I'll fetch Mr Quinnlan,' the assistant disappeared.

'What are you up to, young missie?' hissed Alice. 'You know the answers to those questions as sure as I'm standing here.'

Lauren just had time to explain about Josh's note when a tall man with ginger hair came across to them.

'Can I help you?' he said. There *was* a slight English accent in his speech.

Lauren repeated her questions, received the answers she already knew, and said she would like to buy the hand scanner. As he led the way across to the cash desk, Lauren said, 'Excuse me asking, but were you born in Canada?'

Quinnlan looked bemused.

Lauren shrugged. 'Only that a Net-pal of mine – on the Internet, you know – he goes to Abbey School in Hampshire, England. And he was telling me that an ex-pupil called Quinnlan came to Toronto some time back.' She looked straight at Quinnlan. 'I just wondered if it could possibly be you?'

The man shook his head at once. 'Not me. Sure, I was born in England. There's probably hundreds of Quinnlans here, though. As many as there are Laurens.'

'No, there's only two. Quinnlan's a very unusual name.'

The man's eyes clouded over. 'Yeah, well. I'm not the guy your friend's talking about. I've never even heard of Abbey School.' He started to wrap the scanner Lauren had chosen.

'Excuse me, young man,' said Alice, 'would you mind showing me how that skimmer works?'

Quinnlan frowned. 'You mean this scanner, madam?'

'Skimmer, scanner. I don't really like to pay for

something unless I know how to use it when I get home.'

There was a demonstration system set up nearby, with a hand scanner attached. Quinnlan moved across to it. 'This one is just the same,' he said. 'It's very easy to use. You simply roll the scanner slowly across whatever you want to copy into the computer.'

'And that's anything? Even handwriting?'

'Of course.'

Alice looked mystified. 'You certain?' Ferreting in her handbag, she pulled out her fountain pen. 'Have you got a sheet of paper? I'd sure like you to show me that.'

With a look of irritation, Quinnlan took a sheet of paper from the demonstration computer's printer. Alice wrote down her name in bold copperplate handwriting. Then, easing the scanner across the sheet, Quinnlan input the image.

'Thank you, dear,' said Alice as she saw the result come up on the screen. 'Very good. We'll take it.'

They were almost out of the door when Alice turned back again. 'My pen,' she called. 'Forgot my pen.'

Quinnlan picked it up from where Alice had left it – and immediately looked down in disgust at his finger and thumb as they became drowned in dark blue ink.

'Oh, that dratted pen!' cried Alice. 'Lauren's always telling me to get another one,' she babbled, grabbing another sheet of printer paper and dabbing it over Quinnlan's fingers. 'You don't sell fountain pens as well as skimmers I suppose?'

Quinnlan yanked his hand away. 'No, madam. Just computers.'

Alice smiled sweetly. 'Ah, well. Just thought I'd ask. Thank you for your time. Good day, then.'

'Allie, what was all that about?' said Lauren the moment they were back in the car. 'You know a scanner can read in anything. I must have told you that a zillion times.'

The old woman's eyes glinted. 'He called you Lauren. When you asked him about his name and Abbey School. "As many Quinnlans as there are Laurens", he said. Remember?'

'So? Lauren is my name, Allie!'

'Sure it is. But how did he know? We've never been to that place before.'

Lauren thought about it. There was only one answer. 'He'd been warned? He knew somebody might be coming to ask him about Abbey?'

Allie nodded. 'That's how I figure it. But not just somebody. *You*, Lauren.'

'So – you think that really is the Quinnlan who went to Josh's school?'

'Reckon so,' said Allie.

'But how can we prove it?' asked Lauren.

'This was the only way I could think of.'

Alice pulled out the sheet of paper she'd used to clean Quinnlan's hands. In the middle there was a beautifully clear thumbprint.

12.40 p.m. (UK time: 5.40 p.m.)

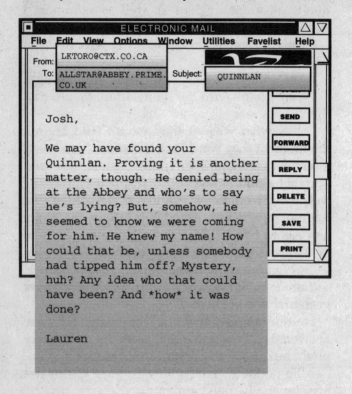

ELECTRONIC MAIL

File Edit View Options Window Utilities Favelist Help

From: LKTORO@CTX.CO.CA

To: ALLSTAR@ABBEY.PRIME.CO.UK   Subject: QUINNLAN

SEND
FORWARD
REPLY
DELETE
SAVE
PRINT

Josh,

We may have found your Quinnlan. Proving it is another matter, though. He denied being at the Abbey and who's to say he's lying? But, somehow, he seemed to know we were coming for him. He knew my name! How could that be, unless somebody had tipped him off? Mystery, huh? Any idea who that could have been? And *how* it was done?

Lauren

Firing her note off to Josh, Lauren immediately started on another. This one was for Tom …

CHAPTER 7

Perth, Australia. Monday 8th April, 3.55 p.m. (UK time: 7.55 a.m.)

Tom sat down at the keyboard for the first time that day. He'd wanted to log in first thing, but half the school seemed to have had the same idea and he couldn't get near a computer. Then, at lunch break, he'd suddenly discovered a dose of homework that needed doing by two o'clock. *That's the main trouble with school,* he thought, *it gets in the way of Net surfing!*

He found Lauren's note at once, his eyes gleaming as he read the first part.

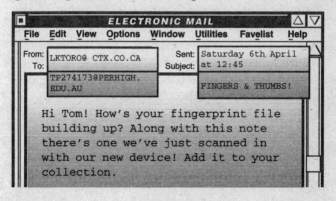

```
████      ELECTRONIC MAIL      △ ▽
 File  Edit  View  Options  Window  Utilities  Favelist  Help

 From:  LKTORO@ CTX.CO.CA       Sent:  Saturday 6th April
   To:                       Subject:  at 12:45
        TP274173@PERHIGH.
        EDU.AU                          FINGERS & THUMBS!

     Hi Tom! How's your fingerprint file
     building up? Along with this note
     there's one we've just scanned in
     with our new device! Add it to your
     collection.
```

Brilliant! Quickly Tom switched to the thumb-print they'd sent across for him. *A loop pattern, clear as anything!* he thought, feeling pleased with his growing ability to identify the different types of print.

Only then did he read the second part of Lauren's note.

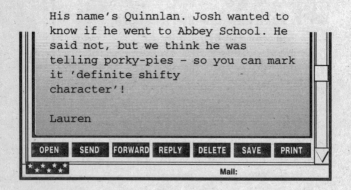

```
His name's Quinnlan. Josh wanted to
know if he went to Abbey School. He
said not, but we think he was
telling porky-pies - so you can mark
it 'definite shifty
character'!

Lauren
```

| OPEN | SEND | FORWARD | REPLY | DELETE | SAVE | PRINT |

Mail:

Quinnlan? Why did that name ring a bell? And then he remembered: the batch of prints Mitch had sent him. He'd said they were of ex-Abbey pupils – and wasn't there a Quinn-something signature amongst those?

He loaded Mitch's batch of prints. Picking out the one he was after, Tom zoomed in on it. The signature wasn't Quinnlan, but 'Quinnie'. A nickname, maybe? But how did the prints compare?

With mounting excitement, Tom opened another window on his screen display, moving the 'Quinnie' print to the right-hand side. Then, into the left-hand window, he loaded the print Lauren had just sent him.

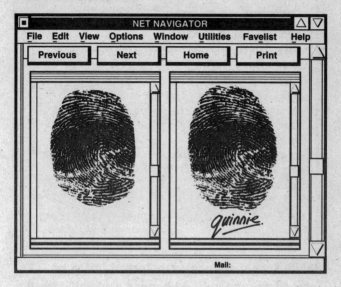

They matched!

These prints *had* to have come from the same guy. Lauren and Allie had been right. The Quinnlan they'd met in Toronto *was* the same kid who'd gone to Abbey School all those years ago. Tom e-mailed the news of his discovery straight away.

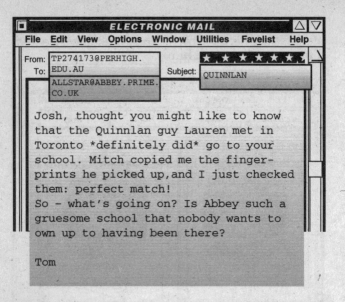

From: TP274173@PERHIGH.EDU.AU
To: ALLSTAR@ABBEY.PRIME.CO.UK
Subject: QUINNLAN

Josh, thought you might like to know that the Quinnlan guy Lauren met in Toronto *definitely did* go to your school. Mitch copied me the finger-prints he picked up, and I just checked them: perfect match!
So - what's going on? Is Abbey such a gruesome school that nobody wants to own up to having been there?

Tom

Abbey School. Monday 8th April, 12.45 p.m.

Josh, Tamsyn and Rob met up outside the Technology Block. Each was holding a copy of Lauren's note, printed down by Josh after he'd read it in a hurry that morning, just before registration. They'd had no time to think about it then.

'Want to go inside?' Tamsyn asked.

Rob shook his head. 'Let's stay out here. The sun's out for once.'

'Over there, then,' said Josh. He led the way beyond the new extension, still with its pile of rubble outside, to the shelter of a clump of trees and overgrown shrubbery.

'Not much left of this lot now, is there?' said Tamsyn, settling herself down. 'They must have cleared away most of it to put the new building up.'

'Just as well,' said Rob. 'It was a right jungle.'

'Can we forget the environment for a minute?' said Josh. He spread his copy of Lauren's note on the ground. 'What about this? Does it tell us anything, d'you reckon?'

Tamsyn looked at him. 'It tells us Quinnlan didn't want to own up to the fact that he came here.'

'But why not?' said Rob.

'Isn't it obvious?' said Josh. 'He was in my dad's year. If that fire was started by *him*, wouldn't that be a reason to deny he was ever here?'

Tamsyn wasn't convinced. 'But – why would it have mattered? He's been living in Canada for yonks. He can't be touched for it now. Why should Quinnlan care?'

'I don't know!' said Josh. 'But if it *was* him, he could have tipped off the others – McGilray and Connie Pasquale.'

Tamsyn looked thoughtful. 'Connie Pasquale *had* been sent a message, hadn't she? She told Mitch that. It was why she wouldn't give him any more info.'

'And if McGilray had got a similar message,' said Rob, 'that could have been why he cut the fire bit from the article.'

'Maybe those messages came from Quinnlan, then,' said Tamsyn.

No! realized Josh. *It couldn't possibly have been that way!*

'Somebody tipped them off,' said Josh. 'But it wasn't Quinnlan. He wouldn't have known we'd get an article put in the *Chronicle*. And he knew Lauren's name.'

'Now *that's* a mystery,' said Rob. 'How did he know her name?'

Josh ignored the question as his thinking leapt ahead. 'So Quinnlan must have been *expecting* her to come looking for him. He must have been tipped off himself!'

'But not with the same message,' said Tamsyn quietly.

Josh looked at her. 'How d'you work that out?'

'Because if he'd been told to say nothing, then that's just what he'd have said – nothing.'

'There'd have been no need for him to *deny* being an Abbeyite,' said Rob. 'Is that what you're getting at?'

Tamsyn nodded in agreement.

'So it comes back to him being the one!' cried Josh.

'One *of* them, maybe,' said Tamsyn. 'But not *the* one. He would hardly have sent a message to himself, would he?'

Rob realized what she was suggesting. 'Josh – didn't your dad say he heard two sets of footsteps on the night of the fire?'

'Yes, he did! So, if Quinnlan was one of them, then whoever tipped him off … whoever got in touch with McGilray and Connie Pasquale … is the other one?'

'The person who seems to have been one step

ahead of us all the way,' said Tamsyn.

'*How*, I'd like to know,' said Rob.

Josh responded fiercely. 'You can stick "how". I don't care. What I want to know is *who*. Who is it?'

Tamsyn pulled a book from her holdall. It was, Josh saw, her well-thumbed copy of Charles Dickens' *Great Expectations*.

'Come on, you're not going to quit on this problem now!' he cried.

Tamsyn held the book up. 'Chill out, Josh. Listen. In this story,' she said, 'the main character, Pip, is being sent money. He doesn't know who by. He assumes it's an old woman called Miss Havisham. But he's wrong. She doesn't like him; she wasn't his friend. The one who's sending the money is a reformed prisoner called Magwitch, who he helped when he was a kid. That's who Pip's friend is.'

'What has that got to do—' began Josh.

'Quinnlan wouldn't have been tipped off by somebody who didn't like him?' said Rob. 'Is that what you're saying?'

Tamsyn nodded. 'That's exactly what I'm saying. What we need to know is, who was Quinnlan's best friend at school?'

Abbey School. 4.35 p.m.

'Josh! Hello, how're you doing?'

Josh looked up at the face peering in through the door of the Computer Club room and shrugged. 'Hi, Councillor Barrett. I'm doing OK, I guess.'

Barrett eased himself onto a chair. 'You don't look as if you're doing OK.' He put a hand on Josh's shoulder. 'I hope it's not what I told you – about your dad and the fire.'

Josh shook his head. 'No, it's not. After seeing you, I talked to him about it. My dad didn't cause that fire, Councillor Barrett. Somebody else did – and let him take the blame for it.'

'Is that what he said?'

'Yeah, and I believe him. Somebody else caused that fire, and they got away with it.'

Barrett stood up, looking thoughtful. 'Are you sure you know what you're saying, Josh?'

Josh shook his head. After their discussion at lunchtime, he'd gone over and over all the e-mails they'd received, looking for any clues as to who might have been Quinnlan's pal. On the screen were the opening entries of the database he'd stayed late to set up in the hope that it might help. None of it gave a clue as to who Quinnlan might have been friends with.

NAME	E-MAIL	SCHOOL DETAILS
Nicola ACTON	No Information	No Information
Geoff ALLAN	**Not on Net**	**Married Tina Kerrens. Son, JOSH ALLAN**
Vanessa ARNOLD	No Information	No Information
Paul BARRETT	**BARRETT@SYSCO. CO.UK**	**96% in Scholarship**
Sophie BRYANT	No Information	No Information
Quentin BURWOOD	No Information	No Information
Catherine COLE	No Information	No Information
Joan COX	No Information	No Information

Maria DAWSON	MDAWSON@LASALLE. ORG.FR (France)	Nutty about Williams. Watched him and Quinnlan in exam.
Gordon EARLY	No Information	No Information
Lucy FISHER	No Information	No Information
Alice FROST	No Information	No Information
Niall HARRISON	No Information	No Information
Mark HUGHES	No Information	No Information
Bob JEFFREYS	No Information	No Information
Mary JONES	No Information	No Information
Tina KERRENS	Not on Net (yet)	Married Geoff Allan
Mark KINDER	No Information	No Information
Vince LANGFORD	No Information	No Information
Anne LEWIS	No Information	No Information
Colin McGILRAY	MCGILRAY@CHRON. CO.UK	Sub-editor, Ports Chronicle
Rhoda MacLEAN	No Information	No Information
Tony NORRIS	No Information	No Information
Connie PASQUALE	CONPASQ@NYC.GOV New York, USA	
Maureen PORTER	No Information	No Information
Ben QUINNLAN	Net: ID unknown Toronto, Canada	Taking exam. SUSPECT NO. 1
Peter SIMONS	No Information	No Information
Rodney SIMPSON	No Information	No Information
Michael STARK	No Information	No Information
Janice THORPE	No Information	No Information
Mary VINCENT	No Information	No Information
Dave WILLIAMS	DAVEWILL@NINTO. CO.JP (Japan)	Didn't think Geoff Allan was type to start a fire. Messed up scholarship exam. 3 took it. Amazed at 96%. Sends news to McGilray.

'That me you've got on there?' said Paul Barrett, smiling as he peered at the screen.

Josh nodded. 'It's a database. I ... ' He

hesitated. Should he share what they'd discovered so far? As Barrett looked closer, Josh decided he didn't have much choice. 'I reckon there were two of them in it together,' said Josh. He pointed at the line showing Quinnlan's name. 'And one was him.'

Barrett frowned. 'Ben Quinnlan?'

'He lives in Toronto now. One of my Net friends went to see him.'

'And he admitted it, did he?'

'No. He'd been warned by someone. That's what I'm trying to do now. Figure out who it could be.' He turned to Barrett. 'Can you remember him, Councillor Barrett? Did he have a big buddy? Y'know, a special friend?'

Paul Barrett thought for a minute, then shook his head. 'No. I remember Quinnlan, now you mention him. Odd guy. Real loner. Never mixed with anybody at all.'

'Nobody?' said Josh. 'You're sure?'

Barrett got to his feet, still shaking his head. 'As sure as I can be, Josh. Now, if you'll excuse me, I'm late for my meeting.'

He went out. Moments later, Josh heard the door of the Technology Block crash open and footsteps racing his way. Before he knew what was happening, Mr Findlay had stormed into the room.

'What do you think you're doing?' he shouted.

Josh was too stunned to answer. Never, in his time at Abbey, had he seen Mr Findlay so angry.

'I thought I asked you to forget about this fire business!'

'Yes, sir, but ...'

'But, nothing, Josh. Now I'm *telling* you. Get rid of that database!'

Josh felt his anger rising. *I'm not going to forget about it. I'm going to crack it!*

'You hear me, Josh?' yelled Mr Findlay. 'Delete that database!'

But Josh's hands darted across the keyboard in a blur and with a couple of swift moves he closed down the system – but *without* doing as he'd been told.

Mr Findlay was outraged. 'Right. You're off the project, Josh. I will not be disobeyed!'

Josh leapt to his feet. 'I don't care! You don't want me checking out that fire, because you don't want me to find out who really caused it!'

Pushing past the teacher, past Paul Barrett who was standing outside the door, Josh ran from the building.

Tamsyn was probably right. Quinnlan must been tipped off by an old friend. But did it need be a *pupil* friend?

All the way home the same phrase kept buzzing through his head. It had only come to him as Mr Findlay had started tearing into him – a phrase from Maria Dawson's e-mail that had first mentioned Quinnlan.

```
Whoever he was, he was into technology (I
remember he got on well with Mr Findlay)
so you could find he's on the Net
somewhere as well.
```

That was what had really made him angry. The thought that perhaps the person tracking their every move had been Mr Findlay himself …

Manor House. 8.35 p.m.

Rob punched the buttons on the phone and waited. After half a dozen or so rings, a voice came from the other end.

'Hello, Tina Allan speaking.'

'Hello, Mrs Allan. Is Josh there, please? We've got a homework problem and he's just the guy to help us!'

'Sorry, Rob. He's out, I think.'

Rob groaned. 'What a pain. I suppose we could wait until we see him tomorrow morning.'

'He's got a dentist appointment tomorrow morning, Rob. He won't be in till late.'

'Oh, no! This homework's got to be in first thing. Do you have any idea when he'll be back, Mrs Allan?'

'Hold on …' From the other end of the line, Rob heard a clatter and the sound of a door. '… He's just come in. Josh! It's Rob on the phone for you.'

'Hi,' said Josh a few seconds later.

'Hi to you too,' said Rob. 'What do you mean by buzzing off when your pal's in dire need of homework answers?'

Josh didn't reply for a moment. When he did, his voice sounded dull and distant.

'I had something to sort out …'

CHAPTER 8

Abbey School. Tuesday 9th April, 8.45 a.m.

The broken window in the glass door of the Technology Block was the first sign that something was wrong. Rob saw it as he arrived, then the shards of broken glass swept into a small mound nearby.

Inside, something was going on at the end of the corridor. Mr Findlay was standing outside the Computer Club door, with the school caretaker beside him.

Tamsyn clattered through behind him. 'What's going on?' she asked. 'Did you see that window?'

They moved on down the corridor – and then saw precisely what *had* been going on.

'Oh, no!' cried Tamsyn. 'Look at it!'

'What maniac did that!' yelled Rob.

Inside the room, one of the computers had been wrecked. Its monitor was in pieces. Its base unit had not just been smashed in, but opened up first. Printed circuit boards were hanging loose, most of them snapped in half.

'When did it happen?' said Tamsyn.

Mr Findlay shrugged. 'Sometime between end

of school yesterday and first thing this morning. During the night, I assume.'

Tamsyn shook her head despairingly. 'I only used it at five o'clock. I'd been in the library, and came in on my way home.' She gazed down at the floor and said softly, 'Look at that disk now.'

The PC's hard disk seemed to have been singled out for special attention. It was in the middle of the floor, and looked as if it had been hit repeatedly with a hammer.

'Have you got any idea who did it, Mr Findlay?' asked Rob.

The teacher didn't answer the question, but said, 'Whoever it was seems to have been very choosy … and very thorough.'

'How do you mean?' asked Tamsyn.

Mr Findlay waved an arm round the room. 'I would have thought it was obvious. There are four PCs in this room, Tamsyn. There are another dozen along this corridor. Only one has been smashed.'

'If it's a case of plain old vandalism, why haven't they all been wrecked?' said Rob. He shook his head in disbelief. 'No. Mr Findlay's right, Tamsyn. That machine's been singled out.'

'But that would mean,' said Tamsyn slowly, 'it was done by somebody who knew their way around this place …'

She looked at the wreckage on the floor. 'That's incredible. It's our favourite PC. It's got the biggest hard disk.'

'Had the biggest hard disk,' said Rob.

'We all used it. Josh had loads of stuff on that disk. Sheesh, he's going to be sick when he sees this.'

Mr Findlay looked around. 'Where is Josh? Do you know?'

'He'll be in late,' said Rob. 'He's at the dentist's. Tamsyn's right. He'll get a shock when he sees this.'

Mr Findlay's face was set like stone. 'Possibly,' he said.

Abbey School. 10:45 a.m.

The morning was constantly interrupted. Mr Findlay's design lesson was held in one of the classrooms along the central corridor which ran through the Technology Block. Through the low-level windows they were able to see out and across to the Computer Club room on the other side of the corridor. Every time Mr Findlay was called away, Tamsyn and Rob were able to see the reason why.

A uniformed police officer was one of the first visitors, taking notes as Mr Findlay spoke with her. After that, the school caretaker removed the wrecked computer and cleared up the room.

'What's *he* doing here?' hissed Rob as they saw Paul Barrett arrive, loaded down with a couple of large boxes.

As the bell went for morning break, Josh arrived. Tamsyn and Rob had no time to tell him what had happened. The moment he walked down the corridor Mr Findlay came out to meet him.

'You've all got classes to go to,' the teacher said loudly, as a milling crowd built up around them. 'So go!'

Rob immediately leaned over the side of his wheelchair. 'Well, what do you know,' he muttered in Tamsyn's ear. 'I can't seem to get this brake undone. Looks like I'll have to stay here for a bit – with you, of course!'

From inside the classroom they heard Mr Findlay explain about the wrecked computer.

'That's unreal,' Josh said. 'I can't believe it. Why'd anybody want to do that?'

The teacher didn't answer his question, but went on, 'Fortunately, Councillor Barrett has kindly agreed to loan us one of his office PCs so that the school won't suffer.'

'So *that's* what was in the boxes,' said Tamsyn. It was Paul Barrett's voice they heard next.

'Do us a favour, Josh. Log in to the Net for me, will you. I want to be sure the communications connections are working.'

Rob released the wheel brake he'd been holding on, and eased his chair out into the corridor. Tamsyn followed. Through the computer room door, they saw Josh seat himself at the PC Barrett had donated and Mr Findlay had just installed.

It was as he was logging in that Barrett then said, 'Any idea who might have busted in here, Josh?'

Josh shrugged. 'No. None at all.'

Then Mr Findlay asked, 'You were a bit fired up when you left here yesterday afternoon, Josh. Were you fired up enough to come back and ...?'

He left the suggestion dangling in the air. 'Me?' Josh whirled round on him. 'Why would I do it? I lost stuff on that hard disk too.'

'You weren't here last night, then?'

'No, I wasn't! I didn't wreck that PC. You should be asking who did – and why!'

Paul Barrett murmured something in Mr Findlay's ear. When the teacher spoke again, his voice was very firm. 'Josh, if you weren't here last night, can you explain how you logged in to the Internet at eight o'clock?'

'What?' said Josh. 'What are you on about?'

Stepping forward from the doorway, Tamsyn pointed at the screen. 'The system says you logged in yesterday.'

The message on the screen appeared conclusive.

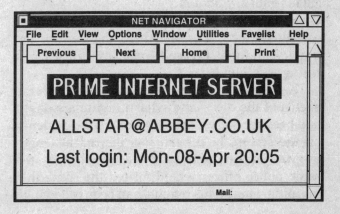

'But I didn't!' cried Josh. 'You've got to believe me!'

'Not when you were at Rob's?' said Tamsyn, saying what she'd assumed.

'He wasn't at Rob's last night,' said Mr Findlay. 'Isn't that so, Rob?'

Rob could only nod in agreement.

'So, Josh,' said Paul Barrett. 'It looks like there's only one way you could have logged in at that time. By being here, in this room, when the building was locked for the night.'

Tamsyn looked at Rob in horror, not knowing what to say.

Paul Barrett broke the silence. Looking at Mr Findlay, he said, 'I think you've found your computer wrecker.'

Mr Findlay nodded sadly. 'I think so too,' he said.

Manor House. 7.35 p.m.

Over eight hours later, Josh still looked completely stunned. 'I wasn't there,' he said for the umpteenth time. 'I wasn't. I was in Southsea, just riding and thinking.'

They were in Rob's room, talking over the events of the day – and what a nightmare day it had been for Josh. Unable to explain the evidence on the screen, he'd been interviewed at length by Mrs Burton, their head teacher, then by the same police officer who'd visited the scene that morning. Finally, his parents had been called in to be told that he was being suspended for the remainder of the week while further investigations continued.

'Now I know how my dad must have felt,' said Josh, holding his head in his hands. 'It's like history repeating itself.'

'Or history being *made* to repeat itself,' said Tamsyn. 'You *and* your dad, both blamed for something you didn't do? Come on, Josh, there are too many coincidences here.'

Rob was toying idly with the keyboard of his computer. 'That time-stamp message ...' he said, thoughtfully.

'Saying I was logged in when I wasn't,' snapped Josh.

'Has it happened before?' asked Rob. 'Given a date and time that didn't square?'

Josh shrugged his shoulders. 'Who knows? You see that stuff come up every time you log in, but you never take any notice of it, do you?'

Slowly, Rob pushed the power button on his PC. 'Maybe that's what somebody was banking on.'

Tamsyn looked at him. 'You – you're saying somebody logged in as Josh?'

'And not just last night. If Josh has been ignoring the time stamps – and he's right, I don't look at them either – then somebody could have been logging in as him for a while now.'

Josh looked up as he realized what Rob's theory meant. '*That* would explain everything! I've been filing all our e-mail replies. Anybody logging in as me would have been able to read the lot!'

'They'd have known about the *Portsmouth Chronicle* invite,' said Tamsyn. 'So they could have nobbled the sub-editor, McGilray.'

'They'd have known about Connie Pasquale's offer,' said Rob. 'And seen our note to Mitch asking him to call on her.'

'Quinnlan!' cried Josh. 'They'd have been able to warn him, too, because they'd have seen our e-mail to Lauren. To Lauren ...' Josh snapped his fingers. '*That's* how Quinnlan knew her name! He'd been told to expect her!'

'And, finally,' said Rob, 'they'd have been able to log in as you yesterday evening.'

'But – how?' asked Tamsyn, running a hand through her hair. 'Come on, guys, tell me how. Whenever we log in, we have to give our passwords, right?'

Josh nodded. 'But if somebody found out what my password was ...'

'That's my point. Even *we* don't know your password! You guard your password like it was the crown jewels!'

'The last time you changed it, Josh,' said Rob. 'Did you write it down on a piece of paper? Anything that could have been found?'

'Leave it out!' cried Josh. 'Anybody knows you don't do that. Man, I even changed it from a guessable word to a random bunch of letters and digits that nobody could guess in a—'

He stopped as the memory came back to him.

'I *did* write it down,' he said. 'After changing it, I wasn't certain I'd remember it myself.' He looked at the others. 'I wrote it down on the back of my hand.'

'When?'

'Tuesday. The morning after my April Fool's trick. Remember, when we were checking the on-line *Chronicle*?'

'But – that was the morning ...'

'When Mr Findlay brought Councillor Barrett round,' said Josh. 'Barrett could have seen it.'

'Councillor Barrett,' murmured Rob.

'Or Mr Findlay,' said Josh. 'Don't forget him. He must have seen it as well.'

'One out of two suspects, then,' said Rob.

Tamsyn looked at him. 'Unless they're in it together,' she said.

Josh got to his feet and looked out of Rob's window. Manor House sat proudly at the top of Portsdown Hill, the whole of Portsmouth spread out beneath it. Far in the distance, the division between the land and the sea showed him the city's resort area of Southsea. And he remembered ...

'It can't be *both* of them,' he cried. 'That's what I sorted out last night. I went for a bike ride, down to Southsea. I'd had this big row with Mr Findlay. I thought he might have been the one who'd warned Quinnlan. But it *couldn't* have been him!'

'It could, Josh,' argued Rob. 'we've just worked that out. He could have known your password.'

'No, it wasn't him,' said Josh firmly. He looked at Tamsyn. 'It couldn't have been. Mr Findlay wouldn't have needed to steal his own key, would he? And he was a new teacher, then. He'd just set up an electronics classroom. Would he have wanted it burnt down? No way. It wouldn't make sense.'

'I suppose not,' said Tamsyn.

Josh went on. 'Then I remembered what you said. Y'know, Charles Dickens and *Great Expectations*? Who was Quinnlan's friend? If it'd been Mr Findlay who'd tipped him off, he wouldn't have told him to deny being an Abbeyite.'

'He'd have told him to say nothing,' nodded Tamsyn.

'Right! Quinnlan couldn't have been tipped off by Mr Findlay. He must have been tipped off by who-ever was with him that night!'

'Then … if we're right about our two suspects …' said Rob.

'It can only be … Paul Barrett? Councillor Barrett?'

'Councillor hoping-to-be-elected-Lord-Mayor Barrett,' said Rob. 'That's a pretty powerful reason for wanting to stop this particular skeleton jumping out of his cupboard. Who's going to vote for a guy who once set his own school on fire?'

'So why go to all the hassle of framing me?' asked Josh.

'To get you off his tail, of course,' said Rob. 'Stop you getting any closer and identifying him.'

'So he's been logging in as me,' said Josh. 'And he's read all of our e-mails since we started this thing. He knows everything we know. To identify him we'd need to have found something that would link him to Quinnlan. That's why I put that database together, to see if I could …'

The answer came to Josh in a flash. It wasn't the fact that he'd been framed for wrecking the computer that was the final key. It was the fact that *the computer had been wrecked!*

'The database!' cried Josh. 'He saw my database. There must have been something in it that he knew linked him to Quinnlan!'

'Did you take a back-up?' asked Rob.

'I didn't have time. The moment Barrett went out, Mr Findlay came roaring in and we had our bust-up.'

Tamsyn gave a gentle cough. 'Josh, your April Fool trick taught me a good lesson. Always take back-ups. When I called in after leaving the library, I couldn't figure out why you'd left in such a hurry.'

She dipped into her shoulder bag and pulled out a small black diskette. 'So, being a good mate, I took a back-up for you.'

CHAPTER 9

Manor House. 8.14 p.m.

'We're looking for a link between Barrett and Quinnlan,' said Josh. 'Anything at all.'

The three friends scanned Josh's database, restored to Rob's PC from Tamsyn's back-up diskette.

'There's not much to go on, is there?' said Tamsyn after they'd pulled out the two entries for Barrett and Quinnlan.

NAME	E-MAIL	SCHOOL DETAILS SUPPLIED
Paul BARRETT	BARRETT@SYSCO.CO.UK	96% in Scholarship
Ben QUINNLAN	Net: ID unknown Toronto, Canada	None SUSPECT NO. 1

'Who first mentioned Quinnlan, anyway?' asked Tamsyn.

Josh looked up and down at the other entries. 'Maria Dawson in France,' he said.

Maria DAWSON	MDAWSON@LASALLE.ORG.FR (France)	Nutty about Williams. Watched him and Quinnlan in exam.

'Who had a crush on Dave Williams – and watched him taking an exam with Quinnlan,' said Tamsyn. 'Surely that's not the link?'

'The whole lot would have been taking exams at that time, wouldn't they? Not just the three of them?'

'But look,' said Josh. 'Look at the entry from Williams.'

Dave WILLIAMS	DAVEWILL@NINTO.CO.JP (Japan)	Didn't think Geoff Allan was type to start a fire. Messed up scholarship exam. 3 took it. Amazed at 96%. Sends news to McGilray.

'It wasn't just any old exam. It was an electronics company's scholarship exam, with a good job waiting for those who came out on top. There were three scholarship students. Williams …'

'Quinnlan and Barrett,' said Rob. 'And Barrett did pretty well.'

'Ninety-six per cent,' cried Tamsyn. 'You're not kidding! I couldn't do that well in an exam if I knew what the questions were …'

Josh's mind reeled as Tamsyn's words sank in. He'd never doubted that his dad had been telling the truth, and that there'd already been two others in the school when he'd arrived that night. But what he hadn't considered was: why? *Why had they been there in the first place?*

'They were taking exams,' said Josh. 'Important exams. So – where would the papers have been kept?'

It was Tamsyn who answered. 'In the school. They'd have been sent to the school, all ready for the exam.'

'An exam Barrett and Quinnlan took, and passed,' said Rob. 'In Barrett's case with a mark so good it was almost as if he knew what the questions were going to be.'

'Which he would have done if he and Quinnlan had got into the school and looked at them,' said Josh bitterly.

'They had it all planned. My dad said this all happened on a Friday evening. The exam was first thing on Monday, so they must have known the papers would be in the school somewhere. So they take Mr Findlay's key ...'

'And let themselves in,' said Tamsyn.

Josh nodded. 'That's why my dad's story about burglars wasn't believed. *That's* why nothing was missing. Because when he turned up, Barrett and Quinnlan didn't want to steal those papers. They just wanted to know what the questions were!'

Rob shook his head. 'But, Josh, you haven't answered the big question. Why start the fire at all?'

Tamsyn agreed. 'Rob's right. They didn't even know your dad was there. Why start the fire? Why didn't they just put Mr Findlay's key back and go home?'

'Think, Josh,' said Rob. 'Go through your dad's story from the beginning.'

Josh racked his brains. *What had his dad told him?*

'He'd had this row with Mr Findlay. About a

soldering iron left on during afternoon break. He wanted to get his own back. So he took a pair of pliers and ...'

'And what?'

'The alarm system!' cried Josh. 'The alarm wasn't ringing!'

'Come on, Josh, of course it wasn't. He cut the wires.'

But Josh had seen the answer. It wasn't in what his dad had told him – but in what he *hadn't* told him!

'No, when he got there! That door was open, somebody was inside – so that alarm should have been ringing. But it wasn't!'

'He could have forgotten to mention it,' said Tamsyn.

'Would you have stood there cutting the wires off an alarm that was ringing its head off?' said Josh. 'Of course not! That alarm must have already been fixed by Barrett and Quinnlan.'

'What, cut the wires themselves?'

'That would have blown their cover,' said Rob. 'They had to keep the whole business totally secret. Any sign of a break-in and those exam papers might have been torn up and another lot set.'

'So how do you fix an alarm without anybody knowing?' said Josh. 'Bust it and then put it back together again?'

Rob's eyes lit up. 'Exactly! That's exactly what you do! Didn't your dad say Mr Findlay taught them about alarm systems? They were bright buddies, Josh! They could have unwired it, got in, then wired it up again. Nobody would have been any the wiser.'

'The soldering iron!' said Tamsyn, snapping her fingers. 'That could have been what happened on the Friday afternoon. Barrett and Quinnlan might have been disconnecting the alarm then ...'

'And that's why they were near my dad's place,' said Josh. 'That's where the alarm control box was. He said he used to annoy Mr Findlay by putting his feet up on it.'

He tried to picture the scene as it must have been that night. 'Then, before they left, they'd have had to switch a soldering iron on again to reconnect the wires. In their hurry to get out, they must have left it on. It must have fallen against the curtains. That's what started the fire. It was an accident – but one they couldn't own up to.'

Tamsyn's short hair shook from side to side. 'Problem, Josh. There was no need for them to hurry. They didn't know your dad was there. As far as they knew they had all the time in the world. And as he didn't come out of the cloak-room, they *did* have plenty of time.'

Rob looked across at Josh. 'Why didn't he come out?'

'Just after I heard the footsteps go by I heard the sound of a police car.'

'Because he heard a police car!' yelled Josh. 'That's why he stayed in there – and that's why they'd have been in a tearing hurry. They'd have heard that siren as well!'

'So Barrett and Quinnlan rush out,' said Tamsyn, 'they don't put the soldering iron back carefully or whatever ... and fifteen minutes later when your dad comes out of the cloakroom, the place is in flames.'

'Come Monday,' said Rob, 'they find your dad's accidentally given them the best possible cover. 'They take the exam as planned – after that there's no way they're going to own up.'

As Josh heard the explanation, anger suddenly rose inside him. 'And unless Barrett comes straight out and confesses, I can't prove any of it!'

Tamsyn picked on the one small fact that was still unexplained. 'Why wasn't Mr Findlay's key found?' she asked. 'Surely they must have planned to put it back?'

Josh sighed. 'Like Rob says. Come Monday, with Dad already under suspicion, they had no need to. Why take the chance?'

'But they wouldn't have known that. I'd have expected their plan to have been to put that key back first thing on Monday, before Mr Findlay spotted it was missing. But they didn't. So – why?'

'Maybe they'd lost it,' said Rob, half-joking.

Tamsyn's reply was swift. '*Exactly!*' she said. 'That's the only explanation. Didn't your dad say he found that door locked, Josh?'

Josh saw what she was getting at. 'Yes, he did. That's why he had to break a window to get out. That's how come he left his jacket behind. Because they'd locked that door again. So they must have had that key with them when they left!'

'So come on,' said Tamsyn, 'put yourself in their position. You're in a tearing hurry to get away. You think there could be a police car coming. Where do you go?'

Picturing the scene was no trouble. 'Into the jungle!' said Josh. 'All those trees and bushes they pulled out to build the extension. They must have been there then. That would have been the way to get out of the school without being spotted.'

'But you've just locked that door,' said Tamsyn. 'The key's still in your hand. And as you're scrambling through the jungle ...'

'You drop it!' cried Josh. 'And try as you might, you can't find it. So there's no way of putting it back. That's why it was never found.'

Tamsyn smiled. 'Exactly. And in the past couple of months that area's been cleared. All that's left of it now is a pile of rubble waiting to be carted away. Right?'

'Ye-es,' said Josh slowly, whilst Rob merely looked quizzical as he wondered where Tamsyn was leading.

'So,' said Tamsyn, 'what if that key has been unearthed by the diggers and is actually sitting somewhere in that pile? What if we were to find it? And what if Barrett's fingerprints are still on it?'

Rob couldn't control himself any longer. He exploded with laughter. 'Tamsyn! Get real! That's about as likely as little green men arriving from Mars!'

'I know that,' said Tamsyn. 'You know that. But

what if Mr Councillor Barrett *doesn't* know that?'

'Then?' said Josh.

'Then we might just be able to make things happen …'

Wednesday 10th April, 3.35 p.m.

Councillor Barrett's car swept in through the school gates.

'There he is!' said Tamsyn. 'Time to go.'

'Happy hunting!' said Rob.

Ducking under the line of orange tape, Tamsyn was clambering over the mound of rubble before Barrett's car had stopped. By the time he'd got out and was looking in their direction, she was on all fours.

'He's coming,' called Rob from the pathway as Barrett began striding towards them. 'Better make it soon.'

Tamsyn waited for just a couple of seconds more then, with Barrett no more than thirty metres away, she leapt to her feet and gave a screech of delight.

'Yes! Yes!'

Racing across from the mound, she was under the orange tape and back beside Rob by the time Barrett had reached them.

'Lost something?' said Barrett.

Tamsyn gave him a look of delight. 'Not lost,' she cried. 'But found!'

And without another word, she was hurrying off with Rob hot on her heels.

Manor House. 5.10 p.m.

Josh met them at Rob's house.

'Did it work?'

'Who knows?' said Tamsyn. 'Come on, Rob, get that machine going.'

They waited as Rob's PC powered up. 'Right, log in, Josh.'

Moments later, the e-mail they'd devised for Tom was on its way.

'OK, Councillor Barrett,' muttered Josh. 'This is one e-mail we *do* want you to read.'

Perth, Australia. Thursday 12th April, 12.44 p.m. (UK time: 4.44 a.m.)

Tom stared at the e-mail, blinked, then stared again. What was going on?

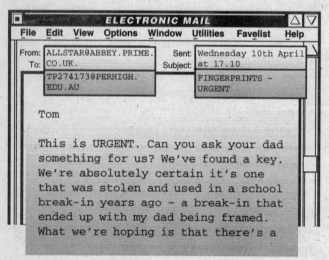

ELECTRONIC MAIL			
File Edit View Options Window Utilities Favelist Help			

From: ALLSTAR@ABBEY.PRIME. CO.UK.
To: TP274173@PERHIGH. EDU.AU

Sent: Wednesday 10th April at 17.10
Subject: FINGERPRINTS - URGENT

Tom

This is URGENT. Can you ask your dad something for us? We've found a key. We're absolutely certain it's one that was stolen and used in a school break-in years ago – a break-in that ended up with my dad being framed. What we're hoping is that there's a

fingerprint on it. If so, we can
match it against the set of prints
for dad's classmates that Mitch
got hold of. He did send them over
to me, but my file got wiped out
somehow. He'll still have the hard
copy, though, so that's no problem.
This is the important bit, then. How
old does a print have to be before
it can no longer be detected? I
won't say how long we need it to be
in this case. Just let us know what
your dad thinks. OK?

Josh
U7W5 JQI3 W743 85'W
523H56-R8F3 63Q4W

| OPEN | SEND | FORWARD | REPLY | DELETE | SAVE | PRINT |

★ ★ ★ ★ ★   Mail:

Scrolling down, Tom then saw the code line.
Still wondering what was going on, he decoded it
so that he could read the hidden message.

'All is revealed!' he laughed.

It would take a little bit of surfing time, but he
could do it. Coming out of Mail, he began working through the menus and down to the 'Crime'
section ...

Manor House.
Thursday 11th April, 5.30 p.m.
They read Tom's reply. It was perfect.

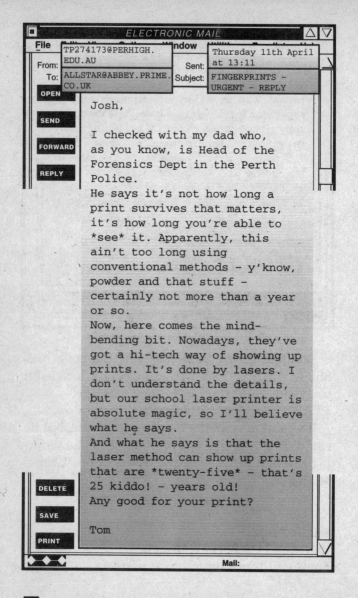

File   Window

From: TP274173@PERHIGH.EDU.AU   Sent: Thursday 11th April at 13:11

To: ALLSTAR@ABBEY.PRIME.CO.UK   Subject: FINGERPRINTS – URGENT – REPLY

OPEN

SEND

FORWARD

REPLY

Josh,

I checked with my dad who, as you know, is Head of the Forensics Dept in the Perth Police.
He says it's not how long a print survives that matters, it's how long you're able to *see* it. Apparently, this ain't too long using conventional methods – y'know, powder and that stuff – certainly not more than a year or so.
Now, here comes the mind-bending bit. Nowadays, they've got a hi-tech way of showing up prints. It's done by lasers. I don't understand the details, but our school laser printer is absolute magic, so I'll believe what he says.
And what he says is that the laser method can show up prints that are *twenty-five* – that's 25 kiddo! – years old!
Any good for your print?

Tom

DELETE

SAVE

PRINT

Mail:

Josh typed his reply and sat back. Tamsyn and Rob looked at him and shrugged. He knew what they meant.

All they could do now was wait until after the ceremony. That's when they'd find out if their plan had worked.

CHAPTER 10

Abbey School. Friday 12th April, 1.15 p.m.

Dropping the pages of his speech on the chair behind him, Councillor Paul Barrett stepped across to a small curtain on the wall. Reaching up, he gripped the short, tasselled cord in his right hand.

'… And so it gives me great pleasure to declare open the Abbey School Technology Block Extension.'

He pulled on the cord. Smoothly, the velvet curtain it controlled drew back to reveal a commemorative plaque. All around them a ripple of applause sounded.

'Nice speech. Not!' said Tamsyn sarcastically.

'Not long now,' said Rob.

As Councillor Barrett acknowledged the applause, Mr Findlay stood up. He coughed slightly, then leaned in to the microphone.

'Thank you, Councillor Barrett, kind words indeed. Ladies and gentlemen, refreshments are available at the back of the room. Please feel free to look around. There are a number of displays of work which you may find of interest.'

The audience began to move about. Tamsyn bit her lip nervously. If they were right, and Barrett had seen their last note to Tom, then there was no doubt what he'd be doing pretty soon – making a bee-line for her.

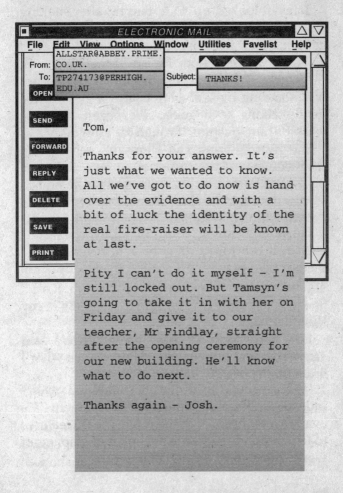

ELECTRONIC MAIL

File   Edit   View   Options   Window   Utilities   Favelist   Help

From: ALLSTAR@ABBEY.PRIME.CO.UK.
To: TP274173@PERHIGH.EDU.AU   Subject: THANKS!

OPEN
SEND
FORWARD
REPLY
DELETE
SAVE
PRINT

Tom,

Thanks for your answer. It's just what we wanted to know. All we've got to do now is hand over the evidence and with a bit of luck the identity of the real fire-raiser will be known at last.

Pity I can't do it myself – I'm still locked out. But Tamsyn's going to take it in with her on Friday and give it to our teacher, Mr Findlay, straight after the opening ceremony for our new building. He'll know what to do next.

Thanks again – Josh.

Tamsyn looked around again, trying to keep both Barrett and Mr Findlay in her sights. She was going to have to time her move to perfection. Beside her, Rob was looking too.

'He's coming, Tamsyn. He's coming over …'

Tamsyn looked up. Paul Barrett, after shaking a couple of hands, was heading her way. He was getting closer. Too close!

'Findlay,' hissed Rob. 'He's over there.'

Quickly, Tamsyn spun round. Their teacher was standing by a display board, a glass in his hand, talking to a guest. She began hurrying towards him, pushing through the crowd.

She heard Barrett call 'Tamsyn!' behind her, then saw, out of the corner of her eye, Rob ease his wheelchair in front of him so that he had to stop. It gave her the extra seconds she needed.

By the time Barrett had caught up with her, she was across the room.

'Excuse me, Mr Findlay.'

'Yes, Tamsyn?'

'There's something I need to show you. It's …' She looked stupidly from side to side. 'It's in my shoulder bag.'

Rob had followed them across. 'Rob,' said Tamsyn, panic in her voice, 'did you see what I did with my bag?'

'Not since you had it in the Computer Room,' said Rob.

'Computer Room. Of course!' She turned on her heel and began pushing through the crowd and out into the corridor. Moments later she was in the empty computer room. Her bag was where she'd left it, on a seat in the corner.

She opened it, pulling out a large brown envelope. Behind her, she heard the door click quietly open.

'I'll take that envelope.'

Tamsyn spun round. 'Councillor Barrett!'

Barrett moved towards her, hand outstretched. 'I said, I'll take that envelope.'

As Tamsyn backed away, he moved nearer. She was cornered. Desperately, she put the envelope behind her back. Barrett's eyes glinted.

'I'm not messing about, Tamsyn. I know what's in that envelope. And if you think I'm going to let you use it—'

With a sudden thrust, Tamsyn pulled a chair in front of him and darted to one side. 'It was you, wasn't it! It was you who got in here all those years ago! You and Quinnlan. That's how you got your top marks!'

She went for the door, but Barrett leapt in front of her. With a sudden lunge he snatched the envelope from Tamsyn's grip. A thin smile crossed his lips.

'Yes. That's how I got my marks.'

'You and Quinnlan?'

'Quinnie. That's right. I had no idea he was as desperate as me. I mean, I'd hardly spoken to him. Then I caught him lifting Findlay's key. Poor sap had no option after that. He had to let me in on the scheme too.'

'But why? Why'd you do it?' asked Tamsyn.

'I wanted that electronics scholarship. A job with the Edison Company was going to be the perfect start to my career and I wasn't going to let anything stop me getting it. Quinnie felt the same, but it didn't work out for him. He wasn't bright enough. Edison's let him go and he ended up with his place in Toronto – a place I could close down tomorrow with the contacts I've got, which is why he'll keep quiet about what happened for ever. As for me, I did well at Edison's ... and went on climbing.'

'And Josh's dad?'

Barrett gave a cold laugh. 'Geoff Allan? Our biggest stroke of luck, Tamsyn. That weekend was the worst of my life. Quinnie knew the fire must have been caused by him dropping the soldering iron after we'd rewired the alarm. That was bad enough, but knowing there was no way we could go back and search for the key ...' He looked down at the envelope. '... This key ...'

'You expected to be found out,' said Tamsyn.

'Not found out. We'd been very careful to cover our tracks. But I certainly expected the exams to be off and the whole class dragged in for a grilling. So when I heard Geoff Allan had been blamed for the lot ... beautiful. I couldn't believe our luck.'

'And you didn't care what happened to Josh's dad, did you!' Tamsyn shouted.

'No, I didn't. OK, it was tough. He just happened to be in the wrong place at the wrong time.' Barrett eased his fingers into the envelope.

'Same as Josh. Like father, like son, eh?'

It was the chance Tamsyn needed. With a piercing scream, she dived for the door. Before Barrett could stop her she'd wrenched it open. Within seconds, a wave of guests and other councillors were pouring out of the extension towards them, wondering what was going on.

Barrett stood his ground, smiling. 'Tell them,' he said to Tamsyn. 'Do you think they'll believe you?'

Tamsyn turned slowly round. Behind her, Mr Findlay and Rob were pushing through the crowd. 'No,' she said. 'They won't believe me. But they'll believe you. And you're the person they'll hear when that tape is played.'

'Tape?'

As a look of horror crossed Barrett's face, he thrust his hand fully into the envelope – and yanked out the tape recorder Tamsyn had set into motion when she'd pulled it from her bag.

'You started that fire, Councillor Barrett,' said Tamsyn coolly, 'and Mr Allan took the blame for it. Just like you wrecked our school computer and tried to put the blame for that on his son, Josh.'

'Come on,' Barrett gulped, looking over Tamsyn's head at the silent crowd in the corridor outside, 'this is rubbish.'

'Tamsyn! What is going on here?' Mr Findlay looked flustered.

'It isn't rubbish,' Tamsyn shouted at Barrett. 'You tried everything you could to stop us finding out more. You even used Josh's password to track what we were doing.'

Barrett was red in the face now. 'Total rubbish!'

'No it isn't,' said Rob. 'That's how you made it look as though Josh had been here the evening the school PC was wrecked! You saw his password. You used it.'

Barrett looked despairingly at Mr Findlay. 'Jack, this is nonsense.'

The teacher looked at Rob. 'What was Josh's password? Do you know?'

'We didn't then,' said Rob. 'But we do now. It was X42ABN6.'

'And I'm supposed to have known that!' snorted Barrett. 'How? Guessed it?' He turned to Mr Findlay. 'Jack, I didn't know the kid's password. You can't possibly believe any of this.'

When he answered, Mr Findlay's voice was as hard as iron. 'Yes, I can.'

He held up the two typewritten pages that Barrett had dropped on his chair after making his speech. Written on the back, as they'd seen him do at the time, was Josh's e-mail address. But it was the short string of characters scribbled above it that Mr Findlay was pointing at.

'X42ABN6, Councillor Barrett. Josh's password. In *your* handwriting, and on the back of *your* speech.'

Abbey School. 3.30 p.m.
'Josh, I owe you an apology.' Mr Findlay sighed. 'We all do.'

INTERNET DETECTIVES

Josh finally recovered his breath. After getting the phone call at home from Tamsyn, he'd telephoned his dad at work. Together, they'd raced all the way to school.

'You owe my dad a bigger apology,' he said. 'He's had to live for twenty-five years knowing he didn't start that fire.'

Mr Findlay fingered his greying hair as he looked at Mr Allan. 'I know that now, Josh.'

'Did Councillor Barrett come clean about it all, then?' said Rob. After the scene in the computer room, Barrett had insisted on talking to Mr Findlay alone in his room.

The teacher shook his head. 'No, of course he didn't. That was never Paul Barrett's way, and he hasn't changed. He blustered on, saying the fire had all been Quinnlan's fault.'

'What about the exam papers? We'd guessed that bit.'

'Barrett was bright. But there was stiff competition for those scholarship places and I'd told him not to hold out too many hopes of getting one. Obviously that was when he decided to make certain.' Mr Findlay hung his head. 'I should have guessed, but I didn't. Maybe because I didn't want to. I was just a junior teacher. Two scholarship passes looked good for me.'

Josh looked at his teacher. 'Is that why you didn't want us to dig into what happened?'

'No, that was because of me.'

As his dad spoke, Josh looked bewildered. 'You?'

'I came to see Mr Findlay just before you started at the Abbey. I told him you were my son, and that you didn't know anything about what had happened in the past. I asked him to do his best to make sure it stayed that way.'

'And the more work you did,' said Mr Findlay, 'the closer I thought you were getting to finding out about your own father! I had no idea you were tracking the real villains of the piece.'

'Talking of the real villain,' said Rob, 'what will happen to Councillor Barrett now?'

'Well, he can forget about becoming Lord Mayor,' said Mr Allan. 'There's no chance of him being elected after this gets out.'

'Will he be taken to court?'

'No chance,' said Mr Findlay.

Tamsyn stared at Mr Findlay. 'No chance? He's going to get away with it?'

It was Josh who answered. 'It doesn't matter, Tamsyn. Barrett's lost his chance of being Mayor. That's going to give him more grief than anything else.' He looked at his father. 'Right, Dad?'

Mr Allan nodded. 'Right.'

'But – to get away with it ...' Tamsyn looked disgusted.

'There is the other small point, of course,' smiled Mr Findlay. While they'd been waiting for Josh and Mr Allan to arrive, Tamsyn and Rob had explained to him exactly what they'd done, and why Paul Barrett had been so keen to get hold of an envelope containing a tape recorder.

'Evidence,' said the teacher. 'You haven't actually *got* very much.'

Tamsyn's scowl slowly evaporated into a smile. 'The missing key, you mean? The one with a fingerprint still on it, detectable twenty-five years later by laser? That's true!'

'He fell for that like a dream,' said Rob.

Mr Findlay looked at the three of them. 'Fill me in, people,' he said. 'If he'd got hold of Josh's password, he must have been able to see the e-mails you exchanged with your friend Tom in Australia.'

'Natch,' said Josh. 'He was *meant* to see them.'

Mr Findlay's brow furrowed. 'Then … I don't understand how you did it.'

'Get ready for a detection lesson, sir,' grinned Rob.

He led the way from Mr Findlay's room in the new extension, down the corridor to the Computer Club room. There, Josh logged in and retrieved Tom's e-mail.

```
And what he says is that the laser method
can show up prints that are *twenty-five*
- that's 25 kiddo! - years old!
```

'Tom finding something on the Net about laser methods was a real bonus,' said Tamsyn. 'That made it all more believable. But the important thing was the twenty-five years. That's what we wanted him to say.'

Mr Findlay was still shaking his head. 'But

how did you know he *would* say it?'

'Simple,' said Josh. 'We told him to.'

'But Barrett was using your ID. He was reading your e-mails, in and out.'

'Yeah, but what he *hadn't* seen,' said Rob, 'was an e-mail from Mitch about a funny way of coding messages. That's because Mitch hadn't sent that note to Josh, he'd sent it to *me*. There was no way Barrett could get at it from Josh's ID.'

'So at the bottom of *our* e-mail to Tom, we'd added a little extra ...' said Josh. He retrieved the note from his mail log.

'There.' He pointed to the coded message.

```
Josh

U7W5 JQI3 W743 85'W 523H56-R8F3 63Q4W
```

Explaining as he typed, Josh converted the message.

'There you go, Mr Findlay,' said Josh. 'The power of the Net!'

On the screen was the message Tom had seen, and acted on when composing his reply.

```
JUST MAKE SURE IT'S TWENTY-FIVE YEARS
```

OFF